First paperback edition: July 2025

Book cover by Flux-1

ISBN   978-1-9680274-5-2 (6x9 paperback)
ISBN   978-1-9680274-6-9 (6x9 hardback)

The Survivor's Apocalypse

Part I
Compound Doctrine

M.P. Hendy

Table of Contents

Chapter 1:

A Survivor's Vindication

The air was thick with the stench of must and stale air. Makeshift barricades of overturned desks and mattresses littered the hallways. Junior, fueled by a righteous fury, moved with a silent, predatory grace, his eyes scanning every corner. Darrel, nimble and quick-witted, followed close behind. "Room's clear," Junior murmured, emerging from what was once a supply closet. The shelves were stripped bare, the only remnants being scattered wrappers and the lingering scent of stale food. "Just rats." Darrel grimaced. "Figures. Davis probably ate all the good stuff himself."

They moved on, kicking open the door to what appeared to be a former dormitory room. Bunk beds lined the walls, most stripped of their mattresses. A single, flickering candle cast long, dancing shadows, revealing graffiti etched into the walls – desperate pleas for help, angry curses, and crude drawings. "Another dead end," Darrel sighed, running a hand through his hair. "This place is a ghost town. You think they skipped out?"

Junior's expression remained impassive. "Davis isn't the type to run. He's a bully. He thrives on control. He'll be here, waiting for someone to challenge him." They continued their methodical search, their footsteps echoing through the desolate corridors. Room after room yielded nothing but discarded uniforms, tattered magazines, and the lingering feeling of despair.

When they finally made it downstairs to the Cadre overnight rooms, Junior held up a hand, signaling Darrel to stop. He pointed to a door slightly ajar, a faint sliver of light spilling out into the corridor. The muffled sound of shuffling reached their ears. "Sounds like a party," Darrel whispered, a sardonic grin spreading across his face. "Let's crash it."

Junior nodded, silently motioning for Darrel to take the left side of the door while he took the right. Junior simply pushed the door open. The room was dimly lit, the only source of illumination being a small battery powered lantern, sitting on a table in the center. Davis, his face flushed and greasy, was perched on a stool, stuffing his face with what appeared to be the beef enchilada portion of the MRE. Jacobs, his loyal lackey, lay asleep on a nearby bunk, his M17 pistol clutched loosely in his hand.

The flickering lantern light danced across Davis's face, highlighting the slick arrogance plastered across his features. He tossed the half-eaten enchilada onto the table, the sound echoing in the confined space. "Well, well, well," Davis drawled, his voice thick with mock surprise. "Look what the cat dragged in. Junior. Back for more, are we? Brought your little friend this time, huh?" He gave Darrel a dismissive once-over, his eyes lingering on the younger man with a flicker of disdain. "How's your daddy's basement doing? Still playing soldier I see."

Junior's eyes, typically bright with humor, were now cold, hard chips of obsidian. "Don't bother waking up

Jacobs," he said. "Let him sleep a while longer." Davis chuckled, a harsh, grating sound. He leaned back on the stool, a picture of unconcerned dominance. "Oh, really? And what exactly are you here for, Junior? Come to preach about how great your father is? Still trying to play hero?" He gestured dismissively with a hand. "Look around you, Junior. This is the real world. Your little prepper prince fantasies don't mean jack shit out here. You think you're so tough? You're just playing soldier in your daddy's basement."

"I'm not here to argue, Davis," Junior said, his voice still deceptively calm. "I'm just here to take something, then I'll be on my way." Davis arched an eyebrow, a smirk playing on his lips. "Oh? And what's that, Junior? Still think you can just walk in here and take whatever you want? You think you can take anything from me?" He punctuated the question with a short, barking laugh.

Junior took a step forward, closing the distance between them. The lantern light cast his face in stark relief, highlighting the grim determination etched into every line. His voice, still low, still calm, took on a chilling edge that made the hairs on Darrel's neck stand on end. "I've come to take your balls," Junior said, each word deliberate, precise.

Davis's smirk faltered, replaced by a flicker of genuine surprise. He blinked, as if unsure he'd heard correctly. Then, the surprise morphed into a slow, simmering rage. "What the fuck did you just say?" he spat, shoving the stool back, the scraping sound echoing in the small room. He leaned forward, his hands clenched into fists. "You think you're funny, Junior? You think this is a game?"

Junior didn't flinch. He held Davis's gaze, his expression unwavering. "I assure you, Davis, I've never been more serious." He paused, letting the words sink in. "See, I've been thinking about this for a while. About how you treat people. About how you hoard resources. About how you... abuse your position." He took another step closer, and Davis recoiled. "And I've decided that you don't deserve to have the things that make you a man."

"You touch me," Davis growled, his voice a low rumble of fury, "and I'll kill you. I swear to God, Junior, I'll rip your fucking heart out." Junior smiled. "No Davis, we've been over this. I'm going to take your balls, remember? I'm going to rip them off with my bare hands." He paused, tilting his head slightly, as if considering a particularly complex problem.

"But you know, I've been thinking some more," Junior continued, his voice conversational, almost friendly. "Taking your balls... that's just the start, really. It's a good opening act, a real attention-getter, but it doesn't solve the problem, does it? It doesn't stop you from hurting people." Davis's face reddening. "You're insane! You think you can just... threaten me like this? I have men! I have..." Junior held up a finger, shushing him. "Jacobs, remember? He's sleeping. Trust me, you don't want him to wake up."

"After I take your balls," Junior said, his voice laced with a chillingly clinical detachment, "I'm going to take your hands. I want you to feel the helplessness as you realize you can no longer hold a weapon, no longer hurt anyone." Davis's breath came in ragged gasps. He tried to back away, but Junior held him in place with an unnerving stillness. "Then," Junior continued, his voice a hypnotic drone, "I'm going to take your feet."

Sweat beaded on Davis's forehead. His eyes darted around the room, searching for an escape that wasn't there. "You… you can't do this," he stammered, his voice cracking. Junior's smile widened, revealing a flash of teeth. "Oh, but I can, Davis. I can, and I will. I pinky promise." Suddenly, a groggy voice cut through the tension. "What the hell's going on?"

Jacobs, bleary-eyed and disoriented, was sitting up on his bunk, rubbing the sleep from his eyes. He squinted at the scene before him. "Jacobs," Davis croaked. "Get him! Get him now!" Before Jacobs could even fully register the command, never mind lift his pistol, Junior moved with blinding speed. A swift kick sent Jacobs' M17 skittering across the concrete floor. In one fluid motion, Junior drew his own sidearm, his X-Ten. He didn't even glance at Jacobs. His focus remained solely on Davis, a predator locking onto its prey.

"Jacobs, sweetie, go back to sleep. This doesn't concern you," Junior said, his voice dangerously soft. The threat was implicit, unspoken, but clear as a bell. Junior continued as if he had never been interrupted. "Where were we?"

But before Junior could make another move, the door creaked open, revealing Darrel, his eyes narrowed, his own weapon leveled directly at Jacobs. Jacobs froze, his eyes wide with a mix of confusion and terror. He looked from Davis, whose face was a mask of impotent rage, to Junior, whose expression was unreadable, and finally to Darrel, who stood his ground, a small but formidable barrier. He knew he was outmatched. Badly.

The room was silent again, save for the shallow, panicked breaths of Davis. Junior remained focused on Davis. "Good job, Darrel. Much appreciated," Junior said smoothly, never taking his eyes off Davis for even a split second. "Now, Davis, where were we? Ah, yes. The pinky promise."

"See, Davis, the thing about promises... especially pinky promises... is that they must be kept. And I always keep my promises." Junior stopped just inches from Davis face, close enough for Davis to feel his breath on his skin. "You can either make this easy on yourself. Or you can make this painful. But you are going to pay for what you did here. You hurt my friends, and that's something I simply cannot tolerate."

Davis, fueled by adrenaline and cornered desperation, lunged. He was quick, but Junior was quicker. He sidestepped the clumsy attack with ease, his hand flying out to grip Davis's throat. Davis gagged, his eyes widening in terror as Junior's grip tightened. He clawed at Junior's arm, but his strength was no match.

With his other hand, Junior reached down, his fingers finding purchase on the front of Davis's pants. A chilling smile spread across Junior's face. "Remember what you did to Emma, Davis? I am going to teach you a lesson that you will never forget. Not that you'll have much time to remember it." With one swift, brutal motion, Junior ripped downward. The fabric tore, and a scream, a primal, agonizing scream, ripped from Davis's throat, echoing through the barrack.

Jacobs, still frozen in place, whimpered and averted his eyes, bile rising in his throat. Darrel remained impassive, his gun trained steadily on Jacobs, ensuring he wouldn't interfere. Junior released Davis, who crumpled to the floor, clutching at his ruined groin, writhing in unimaginable agony. The air was thick with the metallic scent of blood and the stench of fear.

"That," Junior said, his voice cold and devoid of emotion, "is for Emma. And for Marshall, and Kurt. And for every single person you abused and terrorized." The screams, raw and primal, tore through the thin walls of the barracks. Ryan and Daniels stumbled into the room, their faces pale and drawn, driven by a morbid curiosity that quickly turned to revulsion. The sight that greeted them sent torrents of vomit spewing onto the already soiled floor. Davis, a crumpled heap of broken masculinity, writhed in agony, his hands stained in his own blood.

Junior reached down, as if to help Davis to his feet. He grabbed Davis's hand, a mockery of compassion on his face. "Get up, Davis," Junior said, his voice deceptively gentle. He gripped his wrist with his other hand and, with a sickening crack, twisted Davis's hand free from his arm, the bones snapping as he detached it from his wrist. The scream that tore from Davis's throat this time was even more horrifying than before, a sound that seemed to claw at the very air itself.

Jacobs finally found his voice, a choked sob escaping his lips. "Please… Junior… stop! He's… he's had enough!" Junior silenced Jacobs with a sharp hiss, finger pressed firmly to his lips. The gesture was chilling, a silent promise of what awaited anyone who dared to interrupt his justice. His eyes, usually crinkled in a smile, were now glacial chips of ice, reflecting the brutal efficiency with which he was dispensing punishment.

He repositioned himself, his combat boots scuffing against the concrete floor. He placed a boot firmly on Davis's left elbow, pinning his arm to the ground. Davis's eyes, wide with unspeakable horror, locked onto Junior's. He understood, with a clarity that surpassed even the searing pain, what was about to happen. A silent plea for mercy, a desperate, animalistic whimper, escaped his lips. It was ignored.

With a sickening crack, Junior ripped Davis's other hand off of its joint. The sound was wet, visceral, a brutal testament to the destruction of bone and tendon. Jacobs, already teetering on the edge, finally succumbed. He convulsed, spewing the contents of his stomach down the front of his own shirt, the stench adding another layer to the already suffocating atmosphere of horror. His eyes were squeezed shut, wishing desperately to unsee what he had just witnessed.

Junior, however, was unfazed. He released Davis's hand, letting it flop uselessly to the ground. He straightened, his gaze sweeping over the assembled witnesses: the petrified Jacobs, the retching Ryan and Daniels, and the ever-vigilant Darrel, who remained a silent, deadly sentinel. "Anyone else have a problem understanding the consequences of abusing the helpless?" Junior asked, his voice dangerously low. The silence was deafening.

He turned his attention back to Davis, who was now a quivering mass of ruined flesh and shattered bone, gasping for air like a landed fish. Junior knelt beside him, his face inches from Davis's. "You liked control, Davis? You liked power? You liked making people suffer?" Junior's voice was soft, almost conversational, but laced with a venom that was far more terrifying than any scream. "Well, here's a little taste of helplessness."

He shifted his weight, his combat boot now resting firmly on Davis's left leg, just above the knee. The pressure was subtle, but Davis flinched, a guttural moan escaping his lips. Junior reached down, his gloved hand gripping Davis's boot. He paused, his eyes meeting Davis's, a silent promise of pain flickering in their depths. With a sharp, decisive twist, Junior detached Davis's entire foot at the ankle. The sound was sickeningly mechanical, a crunch of cartilage and the tearing of ligaments. The barracks floor was pooling with blood, the metallic scent intensifying.

Ryan and Daniels, unable to bear witness any longer, erupted from their frozen postures. They scrambled to their feet, tripping over themselves in their desperate flight. They didn't even spare a glance at Davis, their only thought escaping the confines of the room and the horrors within.

Their pounding footsteps echoing in the distance. Junior watched them go, a flicker of disdain in his eyes. Cowards.

Junior's gaze returned to Davis, who had finally succumbed to unconsciousness. He seemed to have lost interest. Without another word, Junior kneeled and twisted the unconscious Davis's other foot off at the ankle. Junior stood up, wiping his hands on his tactical pants, a gesture that seemed almost... domestic. The carnage surrounding him painted a starkly different picture. He then turned to Darrel, placing a firm hand on the younger man's shoulder.

"Finish him, Darrel," Junior said, his voice devoid of emotion. Darrel, his face set in a grim mask, didn't hesitate. He'd been ready for this moment since he'd first seen the fear in the eyes of the rescued recruits. He'd seen the haunted look on Emma's face, the despair clinging to Reagan and Callie like a shroud. Davis wasn't just a bully; he was a predator.

Jacobs, meanwhile, was a pathetic mess. He was a broken, whimpering shell of a man, the bile still clinging to his uniform. He hadn't even registered the departure of Ryan and Daniels. His world had shrunk to the horrifying reality unfolding before him. He was beyond pleas, beyond bargaining, beyond even coherent thought. He simply sobbed, a guttural, animalistic sound of pure terror.

Before Jacobs could even begin to process the implications of Junior's words, Darrel pulled the trigger. There was a sharp crack, and Jacobs' sobbing ceased abruptly. His body twitched once, then lay still, a small crimson bloom blossoming on the front of his head.

Darrel lowered the pistol, the acrid smell of gunpowder filling the air. "Good riddance," Darrel muttered, more to himself than to Junior, the echo of the gunshot still ringing in his ears. He took a deep breath, trying to dispel the metallic tang that clung to the back of his throat. He'd expected… something. A sense of satisfaction, maybe. But all he felt was a hollow weariness.

Junior clapped him on the shoulder, the gesture surprisingly light considering the heavy things they'd just done. "Let's get the ladies home, Darrel. They probably want a hot meal, a warm shower, and a good night's rest." A hint of a smile tugged at Junior's lips, a stark contrast to the cold efficiency he'd displayed moments ago.

Darrel nodded, the weight of the situation slowly giving way to a burgeoning sense of relief. He shoved the pistol into his holster, the cold steel a grim reminder of the world outside the ranch. "Yeah, you're right. They deserve that much, at least." As they walked out, Junior closed the door behind them, effectively sealing away the horrors within.

"You okay, Darrel?" Junior asked, his voice low as they ascended the stairs of the abandoned barracks. Darrel shrugged, shoving his hands in his pockets. "Yeah, just... a lot, you know? Never thought I'd be... doing that." He trailed off, unable to bring himself to voice the act, the deed, the finality of it all. Junior chuckled softly, "Welcome to the apocalypse, my friend. It has a funny way of changing your perspective. Makes you do things you'd never imagine back in Mississippi." He paused, his expression turning serious.

"Look, what we did... it wasn't pretty, but it was necessary. We saved lives today, Darrel. Don't ever forget that."

Darrel kicked a loose stone on the stairwell, sending it clattering down to the concrete below. "I know, I know. It's just... feels different when it's not in a video game, you know?" He couldn't shake the image of Jacobs' lifeless eyes, the sudden stillness. Junior stopped him with a hand on his shoulder, his grip firm. "This ain't a game, Darrel. This is real. And in this real world, billions are going to die. We didn't just kill two assholes tonight. We saved three women from a living hell. We brought them back from the brink."

He looked Darrel directly in the eye, his gaze intense. "Think about Reagan, Callie, and Emma. Think about the safety you're bringing them back to. A warm bed, hot food, people who give a damn. That's what we're fighting for, Darrel. We do this for them, we carry this burden because we're men. Now, let's go rescue our women."

They arrived at the barracks room, the door slightly ajar. Junior pushed it open cautiously. The room was dimly lit by a single flickering flashlight, casting long, dancing shadows. "Everybody okay?" Junior asked, his voice low but firm. Susan, huddled in a corner with Reagan, Callie, and Emma, jumped at the sound of his voice. Her eyes widened in relief as she recognized him. "Junior! Oh my god, you're back!" She scrambled to her feet and rushed towards him, throwing her arms around him in a tight embrace. "We heard a gunshot," Susan said, her voice trembling slightly. "What happened?"

Junior pulled back slightly, holding Susan by the shoulders. "It's okay. It's over. We took care of it. Davis and

Jacobs won't be hurting anyone anymore." "But... what did you do?" Emma pressed, her voice gaining a desperate edge. "What did you do to Davis?" A shiver racked her frame. She needed to know. Needed to understand that the monster who haunted her nightmares was truly, irrevocably gone.

Junior hesitated. The details were brutal, gruesome even. He glanced at Darrel, who looked about as comfortable as a cat in a bathtub. He didn't want to traumatize these women further, but he understood Emma's need for closure, for vindication. He turned back to Emma, his voice dropping to a near whisper. He beckoned her closer, away from the others. "Come here," he murmured, guiding her a few steps towards the doorway.

Once they were a bit more isolated, he leaned in, his breath warm against her ear. He recounted, in graphic detail, what he'd done to Davis. The words were precise, clinical, yet delivered with an undercurrent of raw, righteous fury. He described the systematic dismantling of Davis's physical form, the agonizing pain he endured, and the utter helplessness he experienced in his final moments.

She pulled back, her eyes searching Junior's face. He looked earnest, resolute, but there was also a strange, almost detached quality to his expression. Was this some kind of sick joke? A twisted attempt to make her feel better? Her gaze flickered to Darrel, standing slightly behind Junior. The young man's eyes were wide, his face a mask of horrified fascination. He was nodding emphatically, like a bobblehead in a hurricane. His whole demeanor screamed, "Believe it! Believe every single, gory word!"

"You... you really did all that?" Emma asked, her voice squeaking. The improbability of Junior's tale warred with the desperate desire to believe it. Darrel, bless his wide-eyed sincerity, blurted out, "He totally did! It was... intense. Like something out of a movie. I couldn't even watch half the time, but... yeah. He did it." He shuddered, then quickly added, "For you guys! For everyone!"

"And Jacobs?" Emma pressed. "What happened to Jacobs?" Before Junior could answer, Darrel, still buzzing with the aftermath of the earlier violence, couldn't help himself. He burst out, "Oh, Jacobs? He was... uh... well, he was watching. At gunpoint. Mostly. And puking. A lot. All over himself." Darrel punctuated his words with a series of exaggerated gagging noises, earning a sharp elbow from Junior.

Junior watched as Emma, her face still pale but bearing a newfound resolve, pressed a kiss to his cheek. It was a gesture of gratitude, a silent acknowledgement of the ugliness he'd embraced to protect them. He felt a pang of guilt; his actions were far from heroic, more like a necessary evil. He just hoped he hadn't traded one monster for another. "Let's get you all back to the ranch," Junior said, his voice regaining its usual command. "We'll get you cleaned up, fed, and somewhere safe to sleep."

He led the small group out to the Ford Transit. The frigid December air nipped at their exposed skin, making the warmth radiating from the vehicle even more enticing. Reagan and Callie practically dove inside, while Emma lingered for a moment, her eyes fixed on the bloodstains still faintly visible on Junior's boots.

Darrel, ever the comedic relief, let out a theatrical shiver. "Man, I'm never going to look at a box of Jujubes the same way again." He hopped into the front seat, slamming the door shut with a resounding thump. As Junior helped Susan into the van, she looked at him with a mixture of gratitude and apprehension. "Thank you, Junior. For everything." "Just doing what I can," he replied, forcing a smile. He closed the van doors, sealing in the precious warmth. "Alright, let's roll!"

The engine sputtered to life, the headlights cutting through the gathering darkness. As Junior steered the van away from the abandoned Air Force base, he couldn't shake the feeling of being watched. He glanced in the rearview mirror, half expecting to see the ghosts of Davis and Jacobs lurking in the shadows. But there was nothing there, just the bleak, empty landscape of post-apocalyptic Texas.

Inside the van, the heater was working overtime, bathing the occupants in a wave of much-needed warmth. Reagan, Callie, and Emma visibly relaxed, their tense muscles loosening as the frigid air retreated. "Oh, sweet baby Jesus," Reagan sighed, leaning back against the seat. "That feels so good." Callie, her teeth still chattering slightly, nodded in agreement. "I haven't felt this warm in months. It's like... like heaven."

Emma, still grappling with Junior's revelation, remained silent, her gaze fixed on the passing scenery. The warmth was comforting, but it couldn't thaw the icy knot in her stomach. The image of Davis, broken and defeated, lingered in her mind, a gruesome testament to the lengths Junior would go to for the people he cared about.

"So," Darrel began, swiveling in his seat to face the women in the back. "Prepare to have your minds blown. Because what we're going back to ain't exactly roughing it." Reagan, Callie, and Emma exchanged curious glances. Reagan perked up first. "Okay, I'm intrigued. Tell me." "We're talking electricity," Darrel announced with a flourish, as if presenting a winning lottery ticket. "Like, actual lights, not just whatever you can power with a crank radio. We're talking…unlimited hot water."

Callie gasped. "Unlimited? Like, I can take a shower that lasts longer than five minutes without feeling guilty?" "Girl, you can luxuriate!" Darrel confirmed. "We're talking food, and not just the kind that's been sitting in your pockets for three months. And get this… indoor swimming pool." Emma finally stirred, her gaze snapping to Darrel. "A swimming pool? In the middle of… all this?"

Darrel grinned. "Yep. David's got the whole compound set up like some kinda luxury doomsday prepper palace. Private rooms, too. No more sleeping on floors next to guys who snore like chainsaws." He winked at Junior, who rolled his eyes. "And," Darrel paused for dramatic effect, "Bulletproof glass. Whole place is basically a fortress. Oh, and it's 70 degrees year-round."

Junior finally spoke, his voice calm and level, "It's not a resort. It's a home. A family home. Everyone contributes." "Yeah, it is," Darrel confirmed, a little less enthusiastically.

"Chores, patrols, training... but still! Worth it!" He nudged Susan, who was quietly listening. "Right, Susan? Best decision you ever made, yeah?" Susan smiled faintly. "It's... different. David runs a tight ship. But it's safe. And we're fed." Emma spoke up. "David? Is he... in charge?"

"He's the architect," Darrel explained, waving his hands. "He built it all, directs everything. He's... eccentric. In, like, a super genius, multi-dimensional chess kinda way. But mostly, he's good. You'll see." Susan nodded in agreement. "He's got this way of seeing things... of knowing what needs to be done. And he cares. Really cares about all of us." A small smile tugged at the corner of her lips. "It's... comforting. Especially after..." She trailed off, her eyes clouding over for a moment before she quickly recovered. "Just trust me. The past five months have been the most enjoyable and satisfying of my life."

Darrel placed a hand on Emma's shoulder, squeezing gently. "Seriously, Emma. You've been through hell. We all have. But this is different. It's... good different. We work hard, we train, but we also laugh. We eat well. We actually sleep. And the whole... family thing? It's weird, I'll grant you that. But once you get used to it, and trust me, it's way less scandalous than it looks, it's actually kinda nice."

Emma took a deep breath. "So, what happens when we get there? Do we just... start training?" Junior chuckled, a genuine, warm sound that put Emma slightly at ease. "Nah, not right away. Tonight? You're exhausted. You'll get a room, a hot shower, a decent meal, and a real bed. Tomorrow, we'll do the tour, introduce you to everyone, and get you oriented.

It's a bit of a culture shock, I won't lie." "So...are there, like, a lot of...guys there?" She swallowed hard, the memory of Davis's predatory gaze still fresh. "I mean, everyone seems really well-trained."

Darrel, sitting in the passenger seat, laughed, a surprisingly light sound. "Whoa, hold on there, Emma. You think we're running some kind of...Spartan dude ranch? Nah. It's actually...kinda the opposite." He turned to Junior, raising an eyebrow. "You wanna break it to her, boss?" Junior glanced in the rearview mirror, a slight smile playing on his lips. "Darrel's right. It's not what you think. We have more women than men on the ranch." Emma's eyebrows shot up. "Really? How many?" "Thirty-one women, twenty men, counting you three." Junior replied, matter-of-factly.

The van rumbled into the open garage, the headlights illuminating Riley and Andrew, who were waiting with weary smiles. Callie, Reagan, and Emma piled out, stretching their limbs. The warmth of the garage, a welcome contrast to the cold barracks, washed over them. "Riley! Andrew!" Callie exclaimed. "Glad to see you guys," Andrew said, stepping forward to help them with their meager belongings. "Welcome to... well, home, I guess. Is this all that was left? He asked, looking to Junior. Callie shook her head. "There's no one else."

Chapter 2:

A Girl's White Knight

The communal dining room was a stark contrast to the dreary barracks they'd left behind. The long wooden table, polished and gleaming under the soft light, was laden with food. There was a steaming pot of stew, its aroma rich with herbs and meat, a basket overflowing with freshly baked bread, and a bowl piled high with what looked like…fruit?

Callie stared, her eyes wide and disbelieving. Her stomach erupted in a symphony of painful rumbles, a desperate plea for sustenance after months of deprivation. Under Davis's cruel regime, they had been rationed scraps, barely enough to keep them alive, let alone fuel their bodies. Tears welled in her eyes, blurring the already vibrant colors of the feast before her. A sob caught in her throat, escaping before she could stifle it.

"Hey, hey, what's wrong?" Sophia, her face etched with a kind smile, rushed to her side, gently placing a hand on Callie's arm. Olivia hovered nearby, her own expression filled with concern. They could only imagine the horrors these women had endured since they had left Davis's clutches. "It's…it's just…" Callie choked, unable to articulate the wave of emotions crashing over her. "We haven't…we haven't seen this much food in so long." The tears spilled over, tracing paths down her cheeks.

Still reeling from the sheer abundance, Callie finally managed a choked, "Thank you." Her voice was barely a whisper, but Olivia, perched beside her, squeezed her hand reassuringly. "Don't mention it," Olivia said, her voice gentle but firm. "This is your life now. No more rationing, no more fear. This is your home now." She gestured around the room, a silent invitation to partake in the bounty. "Eat. Relax. We'll take care of you. After you've had your fill, I'll show you to your rooms. The bathrooms are just down the hall, plenty of hot water. And if you need anything, anything at all, just ask."

As Callie began to tentatively sample the stew, Emma, who had been silently picking at a piece of bread, suddenly looked up. Her eyes locked onto Junior, who was conversing with Darrel across the table. A hopeful, almost pleading expression flickered across her face. "Junior?" she began hesitantly, her voice barely audible above the chatter. "Could...could I maybe stay with you? I mean... after what happened... I don't want to be alone."

Junior turned his attention to Emma, his brow furrowing slightly in concern. He could see the trauma etched in her eyes. "Emma," he said gently, "I understand what you're asking, I do. But... I don't live alone." Emma blinked, her hopeful expression momentarily faltering. "Oh," she mumbled, her gaze dropping to her plate. "I just... I thought..." "I understand," Junior reassured her, placing a comforting hand on her arm. "But, you see, Olivia and Riley live with me."

The information seemed to hit Emma like a physical blow. "Olivia and...Riley...?" Her head snapped up, confusion and surprise warring in her eyes. She glanced at Olivia, who offered a small, sympathetic smile, and then at Riley, who raised an eyebrow in a silent, "What?" Darrel, never one to miss an opportunity for comedic relief, choked back a laugh, earning him a sharp glare from Riley. "Wait, wait, wait," Emma said, her voice filled with disbelief. "You three...are you...? Like, together?" She trailed off, gesturing between the three of them with a bewildered look. Junior chuckled. "We are. They are my wives, apparently," he admitted.

Olivia, sensing Emma's confusion, jumped in to clarify. "We fell in love with him pretty quickly, and his dad announced our marriage earlier today," she cringed, hoping it was enough. Emma's head tilted, her brow furrowing in thought. After a moment of silence, she burst out laughing. "Wait... you two?" she managed to ask, wiping a tear from her eye. "Olivia, the quiet genius who hoards books? And Riley, the sarcasm queen who hates everyone? You're married to Junior?"

Olivia blushed furiously, fiddling with the hem of her shirt. "It's... complicated," she mumbled. Riley, however, seemed to find the whole situation hilarious. "Yeah, well, turns out I don't hate everyone. Just most people. And Junior's surprisingly good at dealing with my... quirks." She grinned, leaning back in her chair, a picture of smug amusement.

Emma, still chuckling, looked back at Junior, her initial plea forgotten. But the amusement vanished, replaced by a shadow she'd been trying to bury since Miller left. She hesitated, looking down at her hands. "It's... different for me," she said, her voice barely above a whisper. "Davis... he hurt me. He took something from me." She swallowed hard, fighting back the tears that threatened to spill. Olivia's hands flew to her mouth. "Oh my God, he didn't." Emma simply nodded.

Emma finally looked up, her eyes blazing with a raw intensity. "Junior... he didn't just save me like he did for you. He vindicated me. He ripped Davis apart with his bare hands, starting with his balls. He showed me that someone like Davis can't win. That people who hurt others like that can be stopped. That... justice is still possible. He gave me back my power. He gave me hope."

Riley's smug amusement vanished, replaced by a sharp intake of breath. Her eyes widened, darting between Emma and Junior, then settling on the faint, almost imperceptible bloodstains on Junior's clothes. "Oh," she breathed, dragging out the word. "Shit, Junior. You really went there." Olivia, still pale from Emma's revelation, finally found her voice. "Junior… you… you did all of that… for her?" She looked at him with a newfound awe. "It wasn't… just for me," Emma corrected softly, seeing the horrified-yet-impressed look on Olivia's face. "It was for Reagan and Callie too. Not to mention the others that died because of them... Davis and Jacobs were monsters."

Riley mumbled something under her breath, eyes gleaming with a predatory light. "Damn, I would have liked to see that." Darrel, who'd been quietly stuffing his face with chips, choked slightly and shook his head vigorously. "Trust me, Rel, you wouldn't. It was...messy." He shuddered dramatically. "Real messy. My basketball career almost ended prematurely from the splash zone." Junior, who had been silent through it all, finally spoke, his voice low and serious. "They had it coming. And Emma… she deserved to know they wouldn't hurt anyone ever again." He looked at Emma, his expression softening. "You deserve to feel safe." Emma managed a weak smile. "I do. Thank you, Junior."

"Alright," Riley announced, breaking the awkward silence and nudging Olivia with her elbow. "Enough sap. Emma, you're staying with us. We got two spare rooms, and frankly, the more the merrier." She winked, a mischievous glint in her eyes. "Besides, you can help Olivia and me keep this overgrown puppy in line." She gestured at Junior, who rolled his eyes playfully.

Olivia, still slightly dazed, nodded in agreement. "Yeah, definitely. We...we want you to stay. It'll be good to have another girl around, someone who understands." She wrapped an arm around Emma's shoulders, a gesture of solidarity and comfort. "And, honestly, I think we all need a little distraction after...everything." Emma's face lit up, relief washing over her features. "Really? You guys are serious? I... I don't want to be a burden."

Riley waved her hand dismissively. "Burden? Honey, please. We've got David running this whole damn show. He probably planned for this six months ago, stockpiled extra pillows and everything." She grinned, earning a snort from Olivia. Junior stood up, stretching. "Alright, let's get you two settled in. Callie, Reagan, I'll show you to the guest rooms. They're not the Ritz, but they're comfortable and yours for the foreseeable future." He gave Emma another reassuring glance.

As Junior led Callie and Reagan out of the communal dining room and towards the guest rooms, Sophia, who had left to fetch clothes from the storage bunker, hurried after them. "Wait up!" she called, juggling a couple of hastily folded outfits. "I... I grabbed some extra clothes. They might not be your style, but they're clean. And hopefully, something will fit."

Reagan blinked, looking slightly overwhelmed by the sudden surge of kindness. "Oh, um, thank you. That's really... thoughtful." Callie nudged Reagan slightly, offering a small, grateful smile to Sophia. Junior stopped before two identical doors, each marked with a small, hand-painted number. "Alright, Callie, Reagan, here you go. Room 5 and 7. Bathroom's right there," he said, pointing to the door to his left. "Hot water's a luxury these days, but we have an unlimited supply." He grinned, pushing open Room 7 for Callie. "Make yourself at home. If you need anything, just holler. Someone's always around."

Callie stepped inside her room, her jaw practically hitting the floor. Reagan, following suit into Room 5, mirroring her astonishment. After weeks of sleeping on musty beds in the freezing barracks, this... this was luxury. The queen-sized bed was neatly made with crisp, clean sheets. A small, but functional desk sat beneath the LCD window, which was currently displaying a peaceful, albeit simulated, winter countryside. And, perhaps most importantly, the room was warm. A gentle hum emanated from the wall, a silent promise of consistent heating.

"Holy shit," Callie breathed, running a hand over the plush carpet. "This is... a guest room?" "I know, right?" Reagan echoed, turning in a slow circle. "It's bigger than my first apartment. And look at this!" She pointed to the LCD window, still mesmerized by realistic landscape. "They even have… what are these? Fake windows?"

"Yeah, the outer walls are two feet of reinforced concrete," Junior explained, leaning against the doorframe of Callie's room. "Not exactly window-friendly. David's idea, the LCD windows. Helps with cabin fever. We can change the scenery whenever we want. Beach in the summer, snowy mountains in the winter." He grinned, seeing their slack-jawed expressions. "Welcome to the apocalypse, ladies. Texas-style."

He straightened up. "Look, you guys have been through hell. Davis was a piece of work, even for this messed-up world. Take a few days, unpack, relax. No guard duty, no forced labor. Just breathe." Reagan hesitantly sat on the edge of the bed, testing its softness. "A few days? To do… nothing?"

Junior chuckled. "Pretty much. We all take turns on patrol and maintenance, but you're new. You guys deserve a break. Acclimate to the ranch. Get to know everyone. Trust me, it's a… unique bunch. You'll fit right in." He paused, a thoughtful look on his face. "David, he's… well, he's the reason this place is even here. He'll want to meet you. Don't be surprised by anything you see or hear. He's a bit...

eccentric. But he cares about everyone here. Consider him the father figure of this crazy family."

Callie, now bouncing lightly on the surprisingly comfortable mattress, piped up. "A father figure? You mean like… he runs the place?" "Runs it? Callie, he built it," Junior corrected with a chuckle. "And yeah, he's…a father to ten of us. And a husband to nine." He delivered the last part with a perfectly straight face, watching as the women's eyes widened in cartoonish disbelief.

"Nine... wives?" Reagan choked, her voice cracking. "Did I hear that right? Nine wives?" Junior nodded, his expression deadpan. "Yep. Nine. All beautiful, intelligent, and armed to the teeth, sometimes. Don't worry; he's not looking for a tenth. Jessica won't let him." Callie's jaw dropped. "This is… this is insane! I thought you having two was wild, but this… this is a whole other bunch of bananas!"

Emma, who had been silently observing from the hallway, spoke up. "Look, he built this place, right? He somehow planned for all this?" She gestured vaguely around the room, taking in the surprisingly modern amenities. Junior nodded, relief flickering across his face that someone wasn't screaming about polygamy. "Yup, his wives helped. Started planning all this when he was thirteen years old," Junior answered. "Then," Emma said with a shrug, "he deserves to live however he wants. He clearly knows what he's doing."

Sophia, who had been hovering near the doorway, her usual quiet demeanor even more subdued than usual, finally spoke. "David is… a very attentive and fair husband. And all of his wives are wonderful, capable women. They're kind, they're smart, and they all work together." She took several steps forward before continuing. "When you meet David and his wives, you'll understand. Junior was right when he said his dad approaches relationships with a kind of gravity. Everyone here is incredibly loyal and loving. It's actually quite refreshing."

"Well," Junior started, breaking the momentary silence. "I'll leave you to settle in and get cleaned up. If you have any issues in the morning, just look for my brother Aidan or ask anyone." He turned to Emma. "Let's go Emma, lets get you settled in too. If you want, Liv or Riley can stay with you." As they approached the stairs in the garage, Emma noticed the second staircase going deeper. "We're going the scenic route. It's much warmer this way," Junior said, stepping down toward the storage bunker.

"Woah…" Emma breathed, her voice barely audible. "He really wasn't kidding about being prepared, huh?" Junior chuckled. "Dad doesn't do anything halfway. He takes meticulous planning and dedication to a whole new level. Now, come on, Riley's got clothes for you." Emma followed Junior as Riley led her to a specific pallet. Riley grabbed an armful of clothes. "Here you go. Some stuff for tonight, lounge wear, and some jeans and t-shirts. We have plenty of sizes. If you need others, just ask." Riley paused, looking at Emma sympathetically. "Don't worry. We'll find something that fits and that you like." Emma glanced at the pile in Riley's arms, a mix of practical clothing in neutral colors. "Thanks," she mumbled, grabbing the clothes. The weight of them in her hands felt oddly reassuring, a tangible symbol of the safety she'd found.

With the clothes secured, Junior resumed the lead back toward the stairs. Emma focused on the back of his head, the close crop and the way his shoulders moved with each step. As they reached the bottom of the next staircase, Emma stopped dead in her tracks. "Holy…" The Recreational Bunker stretched before her; a sight so incongruous with the bleak reality of their existence that it felt like a dream. The pool shimmered under the lights, the air was warm, almost balmy, and the scent of chlorine mingled with the earthy aroma of something green. "Welcome to the family gym," Olivia said, a hint of amusement in her voice. "David's a big believer in staying in shape, both mentally and physically. He says it's important for morale."

As they descended the next flight of stairs, the earthy aroma that had been a subtle undercurrent in the Recreational Bunker intensified, replaced by a rich, almost intoxicating scent of growing things. The Maintenance Bunker was a verdant oasis. Rows upon rows of hydroponic planters stretched into the depths of the room, bathed in the glow of artificial sunlight. Lush green plants, heavy with tomatoes, peppers, and other vegetables, thrived in the controlled environment. On the opposite side, rows of generators hummed, providing life-sustaining power.

"Welcome to the basement," Junior announced with a grin. "We grow all our own produce down here. It's my mom's project, mostly." Sitting on a chair near the garden, a pair of headphones resting around her neck, was a woman with long, dark hair. She turned, startled, as they approached, her eyes widening in surprise. "Seo-Yeon!" Junior called out, his voice laced with affection. "We have… guests."

Seo-Yeon immediately got up, her gaze lingering on Emma, her expression softening with a deep sense of empathy. She seemed to see the pain and confusion swirling beneath Emma's stoic façade. "Welcome," Seo-Yeon said softly, her voice gentle and melodic. She stepped forward and, to Emma's surprise, enveloped her in a warm, comforting hug. Emma stiffened for a moment, unused to such tenderness, but slowly relaxed into the embrace.

Seo-Yeon patted her back reassuringly before stepping back. "I'm so glad you're safe now. I can see you're carrying a lot. If you want, come see me later. I can give you a therapeutic massage, facial, the works. Help you relax and unwind a little. We can even do a mani-pedi if you'd like. It's not much, but it might help ease your mind, and body." She paused, looking at Junior with a playful glint in her eye. "And you know Junior will be busy training, so I've got a ton of free time."

As Junior continued to lead them toward the tunnel leading to the apartment bunker, Emma turned to him, a slightly bewildered expression on her face. "Is that….normal? Her just, like, hugging me and offering manicures after everything…?" Junior grinned. "Yeah, pretty much. Welcome to the family, Emma. She's always looking out for everyone. She's especially good with people who've been through tough times, and trust me, a mani-pedi can do wonders for morale." He said, then gestured towards the entry way. "This way to the apartments. It's a bit of a walk, but better than braving the cold."

As they stepped into the well-lit, concrete tunnel, Olivia spoke up. "Seo-Yeon is amazing, isn't she? Her sister Tanya is also an esthetician. She does even more advanced stuff, like laser hair removal, and, well…" Olivia trailed off, her cheeks flushing slightly. Riley, walking beside her, finished the sentence with a mischievous grin. "…and other ahem personal grooming services. All the wives are… motivated, to say the least. Plus, with Tanya and Seo-Yeon, nobody's gonna let the opportunity pass."

Emma blinked, trying to process the information overload. Massages, manicures, and…laser hair removal? This wasn't exactly the post-apocalyptic refuge she'd been expecting. "So, Tanya's also… part of the family?" "Yup," Junior confirmed, popping the 'p'. "One of David's wives. Number nine, I think? They all live in the main house. It's… a system. A weird, but surprisingly functional system."

Riley chimed in. "They pride themselves on being healthy and beautiful for David. It's like a competition, but a friendly one. You wouldn't believe the lengths they go to! Plus, there's a community health plan that involves regular physical examinations, hidden under the guise of 'Morale maintenance'." Emma's eyebrows shot up. "A community health plan? So, like, check-ups and stuff?"

Olivia nodded enthusiastically. "More preventative than anything. It's David's way of making sure everyone is at their best. It's not just about beauty; it's about health. He wants us all to be strong and capable." She paused, then added, "Actually, because of it, no one really gets sick. If anyone gets a sniffle, it's caught immediately. They can spot lice, infections, and abnormalities before they even become a problem."

Riley snorted. "Yeah, try hiding a yeast infection from that group. They're like bloodhounds for anything that isn't perfectly optimized womanhood." She winked at Emma. "Think of it as a very enjoyable, very proactive girl squad looking out for each other." Emma chewed on her lip, her mind still trying to process the dynamic between David and his many wives. "But... isn't there, like, competition? For David's attention, affection? I mean, he's got... what, nine wives now?"

Junior chuckled, unlocking the door to his apartment. He gestured for Emma to enter and stepped inside after her, Riley and Olivia following close behind. "Competition, sure, but not in the way you might think. My dad... he inspires us all. Everyone benefits from each other's strength, from their unique talents. Plus, they're all hyper-focused on his goals; securing our future, building this community, protecting everyone. Nobody's neglected because everyone is working in the same direction, working towards the same goal."

Olivia nodded, settling onto the couch. "It's true. We all have our roles, our strengths. "So, everyone has their niche," Emma summarized, still not entirely convinced. "But what about resources? Favors? Doesn't everyone want more?" Junior shrugged. "There's plenty to go around. The storage bunker is practically bottomless, thanks to my dad's foresight. And sure, there are privileges. But those are earned, not demanded."

Olivia piped up, "Non-participants don't have access to the nicer things. Like the pool, the spa treatments, the extra massages. And most importantly, David's approval and recognition." Riley added, "It's like… you get out what you put in. If you're contributing to the community, helping out, striving to be the best version of yourself, then you're rewarded. If you're just sitting around, complaining and not pulling your weight, well…" She trailed off, letting the implication hang in the air.

Emma considered this. "So, it's like a… meritocracy?" Junior leaned back in his chair, a thoughtful frown creasing his brow. He glanced at Olivia and Riley, seeking their input. "No, not exactly. Meritocracy implies a defined hierarchy, a ladder you have to climb. Dad doesn't work like that. Hell, we don't work like that. It's more… organic. Everyone is free to discover and cultivate their own strengths. There's no single path to 'success' here."

Olivia nodded in agreement. "Exactly. It's not about competing with each other to be the 'best' at something. It's about finding what you're good at, what you enjoy, and contributing that to the community as a whole." Junior continued, "Look, Emma, you could survive on this ranch for a quarter of a century, never stepping foot outside and never lifting a finger. Hell, we all could. Dad made sure of that. But that won't help when the world has to be rebuilt. This place isn't just about surviving, it's about preparing. Building skills, building community, building a future."

The apartment, though compact, felt surprisingly spacious. The LCD window, with its idyllic winter scene, banished any sense of claustrophobia. Emma was still reeling, the contrast between the hell she'd left behind and this almost surreal comfort overwhelming. She followed Junior as he gave her a tour, pointing out the bathroom and the larger of the two spare bedrooms down the hall.

"This one's all yours, Emma," Junior said, flipping on the light. The room was simple but cozy, with a twin bed neatly made, a small desk, and a closet. "If you want something in particular, all you have to do is ask." Emma ran a hand over the soft blanket, a tangible symbol of the comfort she'd been denied for so long. "Thank you, Junior. Really. This is… more than I ever expected." Gratitude shone in her eyes. "I don't know how to repay you."

Junior shrugged, a faint blush coloring his cheeks. "Just get some rest, Emma. That's all the repayment I need. Olivia and Riley will agree. You've been through hell, you deserve to be safe and comfortable." He hesitated, then added with genuine sincerity, "And, if you find yourself struggling, or need someone to talk to, we're all here to help. Plus, my sister Lily is kind of an expert psychologist."

The weight of recent trauma pressed down on Emma, but the offer of support, the palpable sense of safety, eased the burden slightly. Back in the common room, Olivia and Riley were engaged in quiet conversation by the kitchenette. Emma, fresh from a much-needed shower, joined them, her brow furrowed in thought. "So…" she began hesitantly, "Where do you both sleep?"

Olivia exchanged a knowing glance with Riley before gesturing towards what was presumably the master bedroom. "Junior, Riley and I share the master bedroom." Emma's eyes widened slightly. "Oh. I… I just assumed…" She trailed off, feeling a little awkward. This living arrangement was certainly…unconventional. But then again, everything about her new reality was.

Taking a deep breath, Emma knew she needed to clear the air. "Look," she began, her voice laced with sincerity, "I want to apologize. Back at the base… I wasn't very friendly to you guys. I… I guess I was just… I saw you two as… I don't know, I wasn't very friendly." She winced, the memory of her past behavior bringing a wave of shame. "I know that sounds terrible, and I'm really sorry. You didn't deserve the way we treated you."

Olivia stepped forward, her expression gentle and understanding. "Emma, don't worry about it. We understand. Social cliques held a power on their own." Riley nodded in agreement. "Besides, everything's different now. We're a family. What happened back there is in the past. We're all starting fresh." "Exactly," Olivia chimed in. "What's important is that you're here now, safe with us. And we're here for you, no matter what."

Their forgiveness was a balm to Emma's wounded spirit. She was finally among people she could trust, people who were willing to see past her mistakes and offer genuine compassion. "Thank you," she whispered, her voice thick with emotion. "That means a lot to me." Taking a deep breath, Emma decided honesty, as Olivia suggested, was the only way forward. "Olivia," she started hesitantly, her eyes darting between the two women. "There's... there's something else I need to be honest about."

Riley raised an eyebrow, intrigued. Olivia maintained her gentle gaze, encouraging Emma to continue. "What Junior did... for me... it was... I don't know how to say this..." Emma stammered, her cheeks flushing. "It made me... I..." She trailed off, unable to force the words out. The vulnerability of her confession threatened to overwhelm her.

Olivia placed a hand on Emma's knee, her touch reassuring. "It's okay, Emma. Take your time. You're among friends here. You can tell us anything." Gathering her courage, Emma blurted out, "I... I think I want to have sex with Junior." Riley's eyebrow shot up again, this time with a hint of playful amusement. Olivia, however, remained calm and understanding. "I understand," Olivia said softly. "You're looking for a way to reclaim your body, to regain control after what happened. You see Junior as a symbol of strength and protection, and you believe that intimacy with him might help you heal?"

Emma nodded frantically, tears welling up in her eyes. "Yes! Exactly! I know it sounds crazy, but... I just want to feel... safe. I want to feel like myself again. I kinda feel like Junior reclaimed what Davis took from me, and I want Junior to give it back to me." The words tumbled out in a rush, a raw and desperate plea for understanding.

"So," Riley drawled, leaning back against the plush cushions of Junior's apartment sofa, a sly grin playing on her lips. "You want to jump our husband's bones. Welcome to the club, darlin'." Emma's eyes widened. "You're… not mad?" Olivia squeezed Emma's hand gently. "Mad? Honey, we've been with Junior for months, and we're still figuring things out ourselves. David's family isn't exactly…conventional. What you're feeling, especially after what you went through, is perfectly understandable."

A knot of anxiety loosened in Emma's chest. She'd braced herself for judgment, for anger, for jealousy, anything but this unexpected wave of acceptance. "But… isn't it bad? That I… want your husband?" Olivia chimed in, "Look, we understand why you feel this way. You associate Junior with safety, with strength, with taking back control. And we want you to feel safe and strong." She paused, her expression becoming serious. "But, Emma, you need to understand something about how relationships work within David's family. Casual sex isn't really a thing here."

Emma's brow furrowed. "What do you mean?" "This isn't some post-apocalyptic free-for-all," Olivia explained. "David takes relationships very seriously. All of his wives… we're all committed to each other, to him, and to the family. There's a deep sense of loyalty and responsibility." Riley nodded in agreement. "It's not just about jumping into bed with someone. It's about building a connection, a bond. David believes in building strong families, strong communities. Sex is part of that, of course, but it's not the be-all and end-all."

Emma chewed on her lip, processing this information. "So… you're saying I can't just… sleep with Junior?" "Not without considering what it means beyond the physical act,"

Olivia clarified. "Sleeping with Junior would mean becoming part of this... this web of relationships. It would mean accepting the responsibilities that come with that." Riley added, "Okay, let's be real here, Emma. Junior is, without a doubt, a wonderful man. He's kind, he's brave, and... well," she winked, "he's a phenomenal lover. Seriously, you couldn't do better if you tried."

Emma's eyes widened, and a surprised giggle escaped her lips. Riley was surprisingly... blunt. "What I'm saying is," Riley continued, leaning forward conspiratorially, "if you're wanting him now, you might as well go all in. Because that feeling is only going to get stronger. Trust me, I know."

Olivia rolled her eyes, but a smile played on her lips. "Riley's point, albeit delivered with her usual... flair, is that you shouldn't waste time wondering 'what if?' or trying to dip your toes in the water. If you feel a connection with Junior, explore it. Instead of wasting time wondering if Junior's husband material, use that time and energy in making that bond stronger." "Because ultimately, that's what matters. The connection you build, the love you share."

Emma felt a flicker of hope ignite within her. Maybe this wasn't as complicated as she thought. Maybe it wasn't just about escaping the trauma she'd endured; maybe she could build a completely new life, a life filled with love, connection, and belonging. Olivia reached out and gently took Emma's hand. "Don't be apprehensive, Emma," she said, her voice soothing. "Don't be afraid of surrendering completely. Junior... he's a bubble of safety and affection. He'll protect you, he'll care for you. And we will too."

In that moment, surrounded by these women, Emma felt a glimmer of something she hadn't felt in a long time: hope. Hope for healing, hope for connection, and hope for a future where she could finally be safe, loved, and truly free.

Chapter 3:

Making A Christmas Miracle

Junior, clad in swim trunks and a Santa hat perched jauntily on his head, surveyed the scene with a grin. Around him, the night shift crew buzzed with barely-contained excitement. "Alright, everyone! Settle down, settle down!" he called out. He gestured around the pool area. "Thanks to all of your hard work, we've managed to pull off a pretty decent Christmas, considering… everything."

Junior continued, "a special thanks to Brian, who put in a lot of hours updating the software and fixing the consoles before they went out." He gave a nod to the married couple. Brian looked uncharacteristically giddy, while Seo-Yeon squeezed his hand. "You guys went above and beyond scavenging those presents, decorating, and generally making this place feel… festive," Junior said, his tone sincere. "So, tonight, after we open these gifts, you're all officially off duty. Relax, swim, play some games, whatever you want. You deserve it."

Noah, Susan, and Darrel exchanged weary but satisfied smiles. The adrenaline of their secret mission to deliver the presents was starting to wear off, replaced by the buzzing anticipation of opening their own. They had spent the last couple of hours tiptoeing through the apartment bunker and up into the main house, carefully placing each gift in its designated spot. It had been a risky operation, dodging

David's nocturnal wanderings and the ever-watchful eyes of his wives. But they had pulled it off, and the look on everyone's faces would be worth it.

Junior clapped his hands, drawing everyone's attention. He handed a stack of brightly wrapped boxes to Callie, Reagan, and Emma, the newest members of their little community, rescued just a week ago. Their faces were a mixture of confusion and disbelief. They hadn't been part of the Christmas preparations, hadn't known about the scavenging trip to Fort Worth, and certainly hadn't expected any gifts.

"Merry Christmas," Junior said, his voice soft. "We wanted to make you feel welcome. Hope you like it." Callie, Reagan, and Emma were overwhelmed with gratitude. The simple act of receiving a Christmas present, a symbol of normalcy and kindness, brought tears to their eyes. Emma, bolder than the others, stepped forward and wrapped her arms around Junior, burying her face in his shoulder.

"Thank you, Junior," she mumbled, her voice ladened with emotion. She lingered for a moment longer than necessary, then pulled back, her eyes locking with his. She rose on her toes and kissed him quickly, but with palpable longing, on the cheek. Junior, caught off guard, blushed and stammered a weak, "You're welcome." Riley raised an eyebrow but said nothing. Olivia, ever the calm and collected one, simply smiled warmly at Emma.

Darrel, Caleb, Noah, Olivia, Riley, Sophia, Susan, and Andrew were practically vibrating with excitement. Even though they knew what they were getting, the anticipation of finally holding their coveted gifts in their hands was almost unbearable. "Alright, alright," Junior chuckled, trying to regain control of the room. "Let's get this show on the road! Andrew, you're up first."

After nearly an hour of childish glee, spewing from the large group of twenty somethings, the excitement finally cooled to a simmer. Noah and Darrel gathered the garbage in separate bins as Susan laid out the buffet. Andrew, who had just returned from taking their presents to their apartment, wrapped his arms around her, kissing the back of her neck.

The recreational bunker buzzed with a chaotic energy. The majority of the night shift were chatting loudly, comparing gifts and sharing stories about Christmases past. Others were already digging into the buffet. A smaller contingent were making the most of the pool, splashing and laughing with unrestrained joy. Olivia and Riley were a force to be reckoned with in the water. Both were strong swimmers and possessed an endless supply of playful energy," their shrieks of laughter echoing through the vast space. Emma, however, remained firmly planted by Junior's side. She trailed him like a shadow, her eyes never leaving his face.

Callie and Reagan, still somewhat shell-shocked by the events of the past few weeks, were content to observe from the sidelines. They sat side-by-side on lounge chairs, their bodies angled slightly towards each other, finding comfort in shared experience. The soft UVB lights warmed their skin, and the sounds of laughter and splashing filled the air. For the first time since arriving at the compound, they felt a flicker of hope, a sense of belonging. "This is... nice," Callie said quietly, breaking the silence. Reagan nodded, a small smile gracing her lips. "Yeah. It is."

Across the room, Caleb was practically bouncing on the balls of his feet, his eyes glued to Sophia, who was cautiously approaching the edge of the pool. He cleared his throat, nervously running a hand through his hair. "Hey, Sophia," he called out, trying to sound casual. "I, uh, got a new game for the PS5. You wanna... you wanna play later?"

Sophia looked up at him, her dark eyes sparkling with amusement. "What game is it?" "It's... it's a racing game," Caleb stammered, his face flushing slightly. "Really realistic graphics, you know? You can customize the cars and everything." Sophia considered for a moment, then a flirtatious look appeared in her eye. "Only if we play in your room. I don't want everyone watching." Caleb blinked. "My... my room?" He swallowed hard, trying to keep his voice steady. "Yeah, sure. My room. Anytime you want."

Before he could say anything else, Sophia stepped forward and placed a quick, chaste kiss on his lips. "Later," she whispered, before turning away and joining the edge of the pool, leaving Caleb standing there, a happy, flustered mess. He almost stumbled over his own feet as he tried to navigate back to the chairs, a goofy grin plastered on his face. He was pretty sure he was floating.

Meanwhile, Darrel was leaning against one of the support pillars, his eyes wide as he took in the scene. It was... surreal. Here they were, in the bowels of the earth, surrounded by luxury that felt almost obscene, considering the state of the world. And yet, everyone seemed genuinely happy. Even the new recruits, Emma, Callie and Reagan, seemed to be thawing out, their faces softening with each passing minute.

Darrel, still marveling at the scene, chuckled softly as Junior approached. "Man," he said, shaking his head, "I've never felt so happy. And it's not just because this place looks like a college pool party gone subterranean. It's... it's the genuine happiness, you know?" He gestured around. Junior grinned, his eyes crinkling at the corners. "Yeah, it is." He paused, his gaze drifting towards the new recruits huddled together near the shallow end. "Emma, who had finally broke free, along with Callie and Reagan, seem to be adjusting well."

Darrel followed Junior's gaze. "Speaking of which..." he trailed off, nudging Junior with his elbow. "Those new recruits are... well, they're new. And maybe a little lonely." He hesitated, suddenly self-conscious. "I was thinking... maybe I should, you know, 'show them the ropes'?" Junior raised an eyebrow, a knowing smile spreading across his face. "You thinking about trying your luck with one of them, huh?"

Darrel flushed slightly. "Maybe. I mean, they've been through a lot. They're probably scared and confused. And... well, Reagan and Callie are kinda cute." He shrugged, trying to play it cool. "But I don't know if either of them would even be interested." Junior clapped him on the shoulder. "Don't sell yourself short, Darrel. You're witty, you're loyal, and you were there when we saved them." He paused, considering. "Here's what I think you should do. Just go talk to them. Ask them if they want you to help them figure out how things work here. Explain the routines, the responsibilities, the… whole David situation." Darrel tilted his head, intrigued. "The 'David situation'?"

Junior chuckled. "Yeah, you know. The whole multiple wives, 'Daddy' and 'Master' thing. It's a piñata of conversation topics for days. See which one seems the most receptive, the most interested in hearing what you have to say. And whichever one that is… well, stick with them. Offer them a shoulder to lean on, a friendly ear. Don't come on too strong, just be yourself." "So… just be helpful?" Darrel asked, a hint of uncertainty in his voice. "Exactly," Junior confirmed. "Be helpful, be funny, be you. Let them see what you're all about. If they're interested, they'll let you know. And if they're not… well, at least you tried. And you'll still have made a friend."

Darrel chewed on his lip, considering Junior's advice. "You think that'll actually work?" he asked, skepticism lacing his voice. He wasn't used to this whole "being genuine" approach. Back in Mississippi, charm and a slick line were usually enough. Junior just grinned and subtly nodded towards the edge of the pool. Darrel followed his line of sight and blinked in mild surprise. There, perched on the side, dangling their feet in the water, were Caleb and Sophia. Their hands clasped together; fingers intertwined. It looked…comfortable, natural, and… unexpectedly domestic.

Darrel's eyebrows shot up. "Wait, since when are they a thing?" He hadn't noticed any sparks flying between them, and just assumed Caleb would just be crushing on her for the rest of his life. "Since… a little while," Junior said casually, as if it were the most normal thing in the world. "They've been testing the waters for a while. Spending more time together, sharing games, you know. Plus, I sometimes catch them sneaking into each other's rooms".

Darrel stared. "Sharing a bed? But... he's actually pulled it off?" If Caleb could get over himself and land Sophia, then maybe, just maybe, Darrel wouldn't have a problem with either Reagan or Callie. He thought to himself, "Man, this underground bunker of love is starting to sound like a sitcom!" He stuffed his hands into his pockets, a thoughtful frown creasing his brow. "So, genuine. Got it. But what if my 'genuine' is... awkward?"

Junior clapped him on the shoulder, a reassuring grin plastered on his face. "Hey man, awkward is relatable! Besides, you're funny, you're quick on your feet. Just don't try too hard. Let it flow, let it happen naturally. We're all a little weird down here anyway." He turned back to the pool, watching Caleb and Sophia. It was an odd sight, seeing Caleb, usually buried in a game or muttering about latency, looking almost...content. He hadn't thought Caleb had it in him.

Bolstered by Junior's pep talk, Darrel decided to take the plunge. He headed towards the shallow end of the pool where Reagan and Callie were lounging, their legs dangling in the water. As he approached, Emma, hanging onto the edge of the pool, spotted him. She smiled, her hair plastered to her forehead. "Hey Darrel! Come on in, the water's... well, wet!"

"Hey Emma," Darrel said, trying to sound casual. "Just gonna hang out for a bit." He carefully sat down on the edge of the pool, a few feet away from Reagan and Callie, trying not to look too eager. Emma, detecting Darrel was here for Reagan and Callie giggled, and decided to return to Junior; "I think I'm going to get out for a few minutes," she said, pulling herself out of the water.

Emma, dripping and leaving a trail of tiny puddles, approached Junior. Junior turned his attention to Emma. "You okay, Emma? You look a little…cold." Emma smiled, brushing a stray strand of hair from her face. "Yeah, I'm fine. Just…a bit tired. You're just going to stand there all night, or are you going to swim?" She gestured at the water with a playful nudge.

Junior shifted his weight, a flicker of discomfort crossing his face. "You know I usually only swim for exercise. Just playing in the water feels…weird." He looked around, trying to find the right words. "It's like, I'm supposed to be training, or doing something productive. Relaxing like this…it's foreign territory for me." Emma's eyes sparkled with an idea. "Well, I could help with that. We can combine the two! I can hold onto you while you swim laps. Resistance training!" She winked. "Win-win, right?"

Junior chuckled, but his eyes narrowed playfully. "Is that just an excuse to get all touchy-feely?" He raised an eyebrow, a hint of mischief in his voice. "Because, you know, Olivia and Riley might have something to say about that." Emma didn't blush, didn't stammer, didn't even hesitate. She leaned a little closer, her voice dropping to a whisper. "Maybe," she admitted, her gaze locking with his. "But it's also a perfectly logical proposition. You get to train, I get to… motivate you. And besides," she added, "aren't you curious?"

"Alright, alright," he relented, a grin tugging at the corner of his mouth. "Resistance training it is. But," he pointed a finger at her, "if I feel any… unnecessary groping, training's over. Got it?" Emma nodded, a sly smile spreading across her face. With that, Junior jumped into the water, followed by Emma, who then latched herself onto his back, wrapping her arms and legs around him. Junior started swimming at an amazing speed, his powerful strokes propelling them through the water. Emma enjoyed the ride, laughing and squealing with delight as they glided across the pool.

As they swam, the others watched from the sidelines, amused by the sight of Junior and Emma playing in the water. Meanwhile, Olivia and Riley sat on the edge of the pool, chatting and giggling as they watched the pair. "I'm glad Junior's finally taking a break," Olivia said, smiling. "He's always so serious and focused on training."

Riley snorted. "Break? Honey, look again. That man is training." She gestured with her head towards the pool. "He's got a fully-grown woman latched onto him like some kind of… aquatic backpack. That's resistance training, Olivia. Advanced level stuff." Olivia frowned, peering at the scene with renewed interest. "Oh. You think so?" She took another sip. "I guess you're right. He does look like he's working hard. And Emma… she looks like she's enjoying the workout. In more ways than one."

Down in the pool, Junior was indeed working. Emma was not exactly lightweight. Each stroke required a conscious effort, and he had to admit, the added drag was a fantastic way to build endurance. He could feel Emma's arms tighten around his neck every time he pushed off the wall. "Faster, Junior, faster!" Emma shrieked in delight. Junior grunted. "Less talking, more drag, Recruit. This is supposed to be challenging."

As they completed their ninth lap, Emma was starting to tire from holding on, but Junior showed no signs of fatigue. His powerful strokes continued to propel them through the water, and Emma found herself becoming more and more exhausted. But despite her physical fatigue, she felt a growing sense of excitement and arousal. Being so close to Junior, feeling his strength and power, was exhilarating.

As she tightened her grip, she felt something inside of her stir. If he was this strong and capable, then she would always be safe in his shadow. She felt her desire to be consumed by him reach a fever pitch. Junior, oblivious to Emma's growing arousal, continued to swim, his focus solely on the exercise. But as they approached the end of his tenth lap, he could feel Emma's grip around his waist tighten. Now, at the pool's edge, the workout was over, but something else had just begun.

Junior, still smiling, his breath even despite the workout, gently pried Emma's arms loose. "Easy, there," he said, his voice a low rumble. "You can let go now. We're done with the workout." He maintained eye contact, a gentle smile on his lips. He expected relief, perhaps a shy retreat. But Emma did neither.

Instead, she moved, her lithe body pressing against his, water cascading down her skin. Her arms and legs wrapped around him, a vise-like grip that left him momentarily stunned. Her gaze, usually bright with playful energy, was now dark, intense, and filled with a hunger he couldn't quite place. Then, she kissed him. Fiercely. A deep, searching kiss that left him momentarily stunned.

Her tongue, bold and demanding, met his. He didn't respond, simply allowing her to take the lead. It wasn't what he expected. It wasn't what he was prepared for. It was, however, the raw truth of her desire laid bare. When she finally pulled back, her breath hitched in her chest. Her eyes, usually bright with a playful energy, were now dark and intense. "Junior," she breathed, her voice heavy. "I... I need you."

Junior, still slightly dazed by Emma's sudden advance, turned to Olivia and Riley, a brow raised in a question. "Well?" he asked. "Why aren't you two jumping in to stop this?" Olivia chuckled, her eyes sparkling with mischief. "Why would we stop it?" She glanced at Riley, who nodded in agreement. "You know Emma's been wanting this. Frankly, she's got guts." She gestured towards Emma, who was now staring intensely at Junior, her expression a plea.

Olivia and Riley, perched on the edge of the pool, exchanged amused glances. The rest of the night shift, scattered around the pool, watched in silence. Their faces a mixture of curiosity, amusement, and something akin to vicarious excitement. Junior, still a bit stunned, cleared his throat, the sound oddly loud in the suddenly quiet space. He looked at Emma, then at the expectant faces surrounding them.

He leaned in close to her ear, trying to keep his voice as low as possible. "Emma," he whispered. "Maybe… maybe not here? I mean, everyone's watching. Let's talk about this later, alright? Emma appeared to consider his suggestion, her gaze softening slightly. She loosened her grip on his arms but made no move to detach completely. Instead, she leaned in and kissed him again. This time, the kiss was shorter, but no less intense.

When she pulled back, he could feel the heat radiating off her skin. She didn't say anything, instead, turning and swimming gracefully towards Riley and Olivia, who were still perched on the edge of the pool. Junior, still feeling the ghost of Emma's lips on his, had sought refuge at the bottom of the pool. The cool water against his skin was a welcome distraction from the raw, untamed desire that Emma had unleashed.

He sat there, the weight of responsibility pressing down on him, heavier than the water surrounding him. He could feel the eyes of everyone, the night shift crew, upon him. He knew they were watching, waiting. After a moment, he kicked off the wall in a powerful, silent burst, gliding across the length of the pool underwater, a solitary figure in a world of his own. He reached the opposite side, emerging from the water in a controlled, silent ascent.

As he took a breath, he pushed his wet hair back from his face and let out a long sigh. He turned towards the edge of the pool and saw Emma, who was now conversing with Olivia and Riley. His wives were both smirking at him. He could only assume that Emma had told them her plans. He knew they were in on it and that they'd likely had a hand in her sudden display of affection in the first place.

He'd resurfaced, the silence of the underwater world replaced by the hum of the generator and the expectant gazes of his crew. And, of course, Emma, a vision of focused intensity poised on the precipice of something… significant. He strode towards the edge of the pool. Riley and Olivia offered him a wide, almost knowing smile. He could practically hear their unspoken encouragement. He knew them, the subtle puppet masters pulling the strings of this particular play. He suppressed a smile of his own. He was his father's son, after all.

He reached the poolside, water beading on his skin. He met Emma's gaze, unwavering, and saw in her eyes not just desire, but a certain vulnerability. A longing for control, perhaps, or a deep-seated need to surrender her own. His father, David, would've seen through it instantly. He cleared his throat, his voice calm, even. "Emma," he began, his words cutting through murmurs, "you've made your intentions clear. And I am willing to accept you." He paused, letting the words hang, as the room seemed to hold its breath.

Emma's face flushed a little, but her gaze remained steady. She hadn't expected him to accept. "Thank you," she replied. Junior's gaze drifted back to Riley and Olivia. He took a step back, turning his focus to them. "However," he continued, his voice adopting a tone that brooked no argument. "Understand this. A declaration of your intentions does not come without consequence." He turned to his wives. "You two were complicit in this, which means your fate will be the same as hers." He watched, carefully, as the implications of his words sunk in, a flicker of surprise in all three of their eyes.

Junior continued. "You will obey every command, every whim. Your bodies, your minds, your very beings…are subject to my will. There are no secrets, no reservations. Any hesitation, any disobedience, will not be tolerated." He paused, letting the weight of it settle. "Do you understand?"

Later that morning, in the main house, David blinked, the lingering remnants of sleep clinging to him. He was warm, nestled between the inviting curves of Elena in his expansive bed, her dark hair splayed across his face. It was an interesting way to wake up, he thought. He reached out, his hand searching for his little fuck-muffin. Suddenly, a tiny, high-pitched voice pierced the morning calm. "Daddy! Wake up! The living room is full!"

David chuckled, recognizing Jessica's unmistakable voice. He eased himself out of bed, careful not to disturb Elena, and padded into the hallway. Already, the smell of freshly brewed coffee was wafting through the house. He found Jessica, petite and energetic even in the early morning, practically vibrating with excitement in the doorway to the main living room. "It's like Santa vomited Christmas," she declared, gesturing with a flourish.

David followed her in, and his jaw dropped. The room was indeed a spectacle, overflowing with an avalanche of gifts. Wrapped boxes of every shape and size cascaded across the floor, stacked on tables, and even placed precariously on the fireplace. "How…?" he began, bewildered. He hadn't heard a thing. Yet, somehow, a small platoon had managed to infiltrate the house and leave a mountain of Christmas cheer.

Jessica grinned mischievously. "A little elf magic, courtesy of the night shift's covert ops team. It looks like everyone on the list might have got what they wanted." "Remind me," he said, his voice laced with a blend of amusement and affection, "who exactly was on the 'night shift's covert ops team'?" Jessica tapped a finger against her chin, feigning thought. "Well, I believe I saw Noah, Riley and Susan training with Grace a lot the past few days."

He looked at Jessica, her eyes sparkling with anticipation. "Alright, darling, let's not get ahead of ourselves. We'll wait until everyone is awake before we dive in. No one deserves to miss this show. Now, what do you say we spread some joy with a little 'wake-up call'?" Jessica's lips curved into a devilish smile. "Oh, I have a few ideas for that, Daddy…"

Just then, the soft patter of feet on the stairs announced another arrival. Caleb, Sophia, and Seo-Yeon emerged from the garage. Caleb had a slightly distracted air, but Sophia's wide eyes and Seo-Yeon's warm smile were both genuinely welcoming. "Morning, everyone!" He glanced at the mountain of gifts. "Wow… Looks like someone had a busy night."

Sophia nodded, her usual quiet demeanor replaced with a spark of excitement. "We're gonna get started on breakfast. Waffles, bacon, the works." As Caleb, Sophia, and Seo-Yeon busied themselves in the kitchen, the rest of David's household began to stir. Tiffany let out a soft gasp, her hands flying to her mouth. "Good heavens! David, what is all this?"

Taylor, rubbing the small of her back, managed a weary but delighted grin. "It looks like we've been very good this year, wouldn't you say?" Summer simply smiled. "It's Christmas morning, and it seems our extended family has outdone themselves." Kayla surveyed the sheer volume of presents. "Remarkable. Truly remarkable. I suppose we can thank the night shift for their efforts." She glanced toward the garage access, a hint of amusement in her tone, as if picturing the troop of gift-bearers.

Soon, Elena joined the growing gathering, her curiosity piqued. She followed David's earlier line of sight, her own jaw tightening slightly in surprise, but a knowing smirk soon followed. "Well, well, well," she purred, her voice a low, provocative thrum. "It appears someone has been extraordinarily busy indeed." Her eyes sparkling.

Then came Jennifer, her playful nature evident as she bounced into the room, her eyes wide with delight. "Oh, my! It's like a toy store exploded in here!" she exclaimed, clapping her hands. She nudged David, her tone laced with a familiar, teasing familiarity. "Master, did you see this? We're going to need a bigger tree!" Jessica leaned against the doorway, a smug smile on her face. "Lily's got a few surprises waiting for her, I'm sure."

Aidan was practically vibrating with excitement as he surveyed his haul. New mechanics tools lay neatly beside several intricate model kits. Beside him, Alissa was carefully unwrapping her maternity clothes, along with a practical candle-making kit. "Holy Moses, Alissa, look at this! This set of wrenches is top-of-the-line!" Aidan exclaimed, his voice filled with boyish enthusiasm. He ran a hand over a particularly hefty torque wrench. "And these model kits… I haven't had time for this in ages." Alissa smiled, gently touching her belly. "These clothes are so soft, Aidan. And a candle-making kit! That will be perfect for keeping my hands busy when the baby comes.

Young Bonnie was practically levitating with joy. Her gifts were a riot of pink and sparkle: a plush unicorn almost as big as she was, a delicate box containing a real diamond ring, and a pair of dazzling light-up slippers. Her father, Eric, on the other hand, was already eyeing his new set of golf clubs and golfing outfit with a more subdued, yet equally pleased, expression. "It's a real diamond, Daddy! Seth's going to love it!" Bonnie shrieked, holding the ring up to the dim light. She then promptly slipped on the light-up slippers, giggling as they illuminated the floor with every step. "Look, I'm a fairy!"

Janet was already meticulously organizing her new gifts: a substantial box of teaching curriculum and a neat stack of stationery. Her husband, Mark, was admiring his new hammock and an impressive tool kit. "Oh, Mark, this curriculum is exactly what I've been looking for to supplement our younger students' lessons," Janet said, her eyes shining with professional satisfaction. "And this stationery! I can finally start writing proper thank-you notes." Mark grinned, already picturing himself relaxing in the hammock. "This is great, Jan. I've been meaning to get a new tool kit."

Marvin surged with the excitement of a child as he unwrapped an X-Box 360 with a generous selection of games. Beside him, Sara was still a bit sleepy but excited about the prospect of trying out her origami. "This thing is in perfect condition, and it works!" Marvin exclaimed, already plugging in the console. "This is awesome, Sara! We can finally have some serious gaming sessions." Sara, stretching, smiled. "Maybe we can shoot some hoops in the rec bunker later."

Josh, meanwhile, was thoroughly impressed with his woodworking tools and instruction books. Lily, however, was in a state of sheer, unadulterated delight. Her gifts were surprisingly... bold: a set of razor-sharp new knives and a rather scandalous-looking piece of sexy lingerie. "Whoa, Lily, you've got some interesting gifts there," Josh said with a raised eyebrow, a grin growing on his face. Lily, holding up the lingerie with a mischievous look in her eye, giggled. "Well, Josh, a girl's gotta have her... essentials. And these knives are beautiful, aren't they? So sharp!" She leaned close to him. "Maybe we can try out my new... accessories later."

Kyle was examining his new hanging steel targets and a generous supply of metal for his craft. Grace, who had snuck in shortly after opening her own gifts, was holding a matching ring set, watching Kyle, expectantly.

Lynn was softly examining her puzzles and a delicate tea set. Her father, Clarence, was surprisingly pleased with his whittling kit, a fishing game, and a brand-new hat that looked remarkably dapper, according to him. "Oh, those puzzles look challenging, dear," Margaret said, already trying out her chair massager. "And a tea set! How lovely."

Parker was strumming his a acoustic guitar while his wife, Jill, was already busy unwrapping gardening gloves, pots for plants, and knitting needles with yarn. "This guitar is beautiful, Jill," Parker said, strumming a tentative chord. "I really thought I would get a knock off, but this is really nice." Jill smiled. "Oh, Parker, these pots are perfect for the seedlings I started in the hydroponics greenhouse! And with this yarn, I can finally finish that scarf for Bonnie."

Scott, enjoying an extended vacation, was admiring his new set of butcher's knives and a pair of durable coveralls. Andrea, giddy as a schoolgirl, was already setting up her new doctor's bag. "These new shoes are wonderful, Scott. My feet will thank me after a long shift. And this doctor's bag... it's so professional. I feel ready to tackle anything."

Carrying his new range finder binoculars, Seth went to check on Bonnie. "Bonnie, look at these binoculars!" Seth exclaimed, already scanning the room. "I can see everything! And my new gloves are really good for grip." He then turned his attention to Bonnie's presents, his eyes lingering on the diamond ring. "Wow, Bonnie, that's a beautiful ring. Is it... for you?" Bonnie smiled as she handed it to Seth, an expectant look in her eye.

Chapter 4:

Snipers on the Hillside

The March air, crisp and carrying the scent of damp earth, did little to cool the simmering tension within the homestead. Noah moved with the grace of a predator, his eyes scanning the rolling Texas hills. Beside him, Seth, his M4 held loosely but ready, mirrored his sentinel's posture. Their orders were simple, unyielding: kill on sight. The raids from the east had become a grim, predictable rhythm, each one a tightening knot in the stomachs of those who called this valley home.

"Anything?" Seth asked. Noah shook his head, his gaze still fixed on the distant horizon. "Just the wind. And a very determined-looking buzzard." He paused, a faint smile touching his lips. "Probably contemplating the nutritional value of a dead jackrabbit." As the two continued to climb the hillside, Noah studied the terrain around him. "Still at it, huh?" Seth nudged him playfully with his shoulder. "Every spare moment," Noah chuckled, a rare, soft sound. "It's... calming. Like building something that makes sense."

His eyes, usually sharp and focused on potential threats, softened as they flicked towards the valley below. Nestled against the base of the ridge. "Besides," he added, "it helps me visualize the threats. See the approach vectors. Plan the... pest control." Seth grinned. Noah's diorama was a testament to his quiet genius, a detailed bird's-eye view of the entire homestead, the surrounding acreage, the winding creek, and even the imposing Blackland Ridge that gave them their strategic advantage. "That's commitment, man."

Seth raised his thermal rangefinder, the faint glow of the device momentarily obscuring his vision. "Hold up," he murmured, his voice low and urgent. "Movement. West side of the highway. Maybe three, four… no, five figures. Too far to see clearly with the naked eye, but the thermal's picking them up." Noah's head snapped towards Seth. "Raiders?" he asked, his voice low and deliberate.

Seth adjusted the rangefinder, his lips pressed into a thin line. "Definitely. They're moving slow, like they're scouting. Trying to find a blind spot. They're not coming straight at us. More like trying to circle around." Noah scanned the landscape through the thermal scope, his mind already a whirlwind of calculations. The highway was mostly a debris-strewn ghost of its former self, a scar across the land. The raiders were smart, or at least, they were learning. They wouldn't charge headlong into a fortified position anymore. They were looking for weaknesses.

"They're heading towards the old access road," Seth reported, his voice tight. "The one that leads to the creek bed. If they get to the creek, they can use it for cover all the way to the north flank." Noah's jaw tightened. The creek bed offered perfect concealment, allowing them to flank the main compound undetected. "We can't let them do that," he stated, his voice firm.

Noah nodded, already anticipating the necessary steps. "Agreed. We take them out before they reach cover." He began to move with a practiced economy of motion, his MRAD rifle appearing in his hands as if by magic. He settled into a prone firing position, before asking. "Distance?" Noah asked, his eyes scanning the approaching figures, meticulously tracking their progress. "Seven hundred meters," Seth replied, his voice calm and steady. "Slight crosswind from the north, about five miles per hour. They're spread out a bit, but their center mass is aligned."

Noah's breath hitched, a common reaction despite his extensive training. He exhaled slowly, a controlled release of breath that steadied his aim. Center mass. Seven hundred meters. A slight gust of wind. All variables he'd trained for, drilled into his very being. He squeezed the trigger. The .338 Lapua Magnum roared, a thunderous report that seemed to swallow the failing light. Seth flinched, not at the sound, but at the sheer power of it.

The first shot was true, as two of the heat signatures fell. Noah didn't pause. The second shot cracked through the air. Another heat signature fell. Seth's eyes were glued to the thermal display, his breath held tight in his chest. He saw the third figure jerk violently, then slump. Noah fired again. The fourth figure dropped.

One remained. It hesitated for a split second, a defiant flicker of heat in the rapidly fading light, before it too was silenced by another precise shot. Seth let out a shaky breath he hadn't realized he'd been holding. "I think you got all five, Noah." Noah remained in his firing position for another moment, the stillness that followed his shots was profound, a stark contrast to the sudden violence. The landscape, minutes before, alive with the furtive movements of potential threats, was now eerily quiet.

Noah was already breaking down his position as Seth continued to scan the target area. "Yep, all five, clean," Seth confirmed. He finally lowered the thermal scope, running a hand over his head. "Honestly, Noah, sometimes I think you could pick a gnat out of a swarm of mosquitos." Noah offered a small smile. "It's just practice, Seth. And a good rifle. And, you know, the fact that they were walking in a straight line, practically holding hands. Not exactly the most tactical approach."

Seth chuckled, a dry, rasping sound. "You say that, but I saw you. That little intake of breath before the first shot. You still get a kick out of it, don't you?" "So kid," Noah said, stretching his shoulders and then the muscles in his back. "They're not going anywhere now. Fancy a stroll?" Seth's eyebrows shot up, mirroring the surprise Noah had felt at his own suggestion. "A stroll? Noah, we just… you know. Made some people spontaneously combust from a distance. I don't think 'stroll' is the word that comes to mind for most people."

Noah finally looked at Seth, his eyes, usually so focused and intense, now held a glint of amusement. "Well, it's a perfectly good evening, and the scenery is… rather picturesque, wouldn't you say? Besides," he added, his tone taking on a more practical, if still strangely mundane, bent, "I just want to make sure I didn't accidentally… well, you know." Seth's brow furrowed. "Didn't accidentally what? Miss? Noah, you don't miss."

"No, not miss. I mean, miss miss. Like, the wrong target, accidentally. You know, the, uh... the unintended collateral. Specifically," Noah lowered his voice conspiratorially, leaning in slightly, "I just want to make sure I didn't shoot any thick Latinas." Seth blinked. Then he blinked again. He opened his mouth, closed it, and then opened it again, as if attempting to process the sheer, unadulterated WTF of Noah's statement. "I... I'm sorry, Noah, your auditory receptors must be malfunctioning from the... the residual atmospheric displacement. Did you just say... 'thick Latinas'?"

Noah's amusement deepened. "Is that so surprising, Seth? I find them... aesthetically pleasing. A certain fullness, a vivaciousness." Seth threw his head back and let out a genuine laugh this time, a full-throated sound that echoed strangely in the vast emptiness. "You're unbelievable, Noah. Absolutely unbelievable. After taking out five... individuals, your primary concern is whether or not you've accidentally vaporized any particularly voluptuous Hispanic women."

Noah shrugged, a casual dismissal of the absurdity. "Well, it's a valid concern, isn't it? One must be thorough. Precision is paramount. And if, in the pursuit of precision, I happen to have preserved some... delightful figures for future contemplation, then so be it." He gestured vaguely with a hand. "Besides, they're rarely involved in these sorts of high-stakes, operations." "Future contemplation?" Seth echoed, still chuckling. "Noah, I thought your 'future contemplation' involved things like finding the perfect load and perhaps developing a more humane method of disarming vagrants."

"A man needs balance, Seth," Noah said, his gaze drifting towards the distant city, a soft, almost wistful look in his eyes. "And I believe that balance is best achieved with a… well-rounded appreciation for life's finer curves. And, if I may be so bold," he added, a low growl entering his voice, "I haven't had my own 'future contemplation' with a thick Latina yet. I'd hate for my meticulous work to inadvertently disrupt my own personal future acquisitions."

Seth stared at Noah, a growing grin spreading across his face. This was it. This was the moment he knew he'd made the right choice in partnering with Noah. The sheer, unadulterated, and utterly ridiculous humanity of it all. Noah, the stoic, almost robotic operative, with a secret, utterly bizarre, and undeniably hilarious fetish. "So," Seth said, pushing himself off a particularly large rock. "You're saying, if you'd accidentally… you know… incinerated a particularly voluptuous señora, you'd be upset because she wouldn't be available for your… personal future acquisitions?"

Noah nodded sagely, as if discussing the finer points of contract law. "Precisely. It's about respecting the… the potential. And frankly, the waste would be egregious. Such… natural talent, you know, going to waste." He looked directly at Seth, a perfectly straight face that was almost, but not quite, enough to make Seth believe he was entirely serious.

Back in the main house, Alissa, Taylor and Jessica, talked amicably as they simultaneously wrangled their children in a play circle of activity. Poppy, the blossoming six-month-old, was obviously trying to articulate complex thoughts, even though her limited vocabulary simply erupting in a series of short words and garbled sounds as she repeatedly attempted to stack wooden blocks on the carpeted floor.

Alissa's son Tyler, watched the proceedings with wide, unblinking eyes from Alissa's lap. Lucas, Taylor's one-month-old son, was nestled securely in a bouncing seat, swatting his fists at the stuffed animals hanging over his head. "She's really trying to tell us something, isn't she?" Taylor murmured, gently stroking Lucas's hair. Her gaze was fixed on Poppy, a suspicious smile playing on her lips.

Alissa chuckled, shifting Tyler in her arms. "I think she's critiquing our parenting skills. Probably judging our questionable taste in toys." Jessica, ever the witty one, added, "Or maybe she's demanding a more robust snack selection. You know, something with more... structural integrity." She wiggled her fingers near Poppy's face, earning a delighted shriek.

Alissa laughed, a warm sound that echoed in the spacious living room. "Speaking of discerning tastes, I saw Junior's wives waiting for him yesterday. They were lined up outside the training room, all silent and expectant. It was... unnerving, honestly. Like watching the Stepford Wives practice their synchronized blinking."

Taylor nodded, a thoughtful look on her face. "They do seem very... regimented. Junior's really strict." "He is," Jessica agreed, a hint of challenge in her tone. "But it's different, isn't it? David carries a different weight. He's got that unique way of looking at things, plus he's already experienced so much loss." She smiled at Alissa. "He's really a softie at heart, our David, even with all his brilliance."

Alissa mused, shifting Tyler again, who was starting to stir, a tiny frown creasing his brow. "I don't know," she confessed, her voice dropping a notch. "Sometimes I wonder if Junior is too strict. I mean, I see how dedicated Olivia and Riley are, and even Emma, bless her heart, but it feels… intense, like he's pushing them too hard?"

Jessica waved a dismissive hand, a playful smirk dancing on her lips. "Oh, Alissa, you worry too much. That's not intensity; that's high-protocol training. Think of it like the most elite private submissive wife boot camp, but… with better skincare. Junior's just building them up, making them the best they can be." She winked. "And honestly? They seem perfectly happy to me. They practically glow. Plus, he even encourages them to spend time with all of us wives."

Taylor chuckled. "You always have a way of putting things, Jess." She took a sip of her tea, then looked at Jessica with curiosity. "Speaking of Junior's wives… if you had to pick, who do you think you like the most?" Jessica tilted her head, considering the question seriously. Her eyes scanned the room as if visualizing each of Junior's wives, tapping a finger against her chin. "Oh, that's a tough one," she admitted. "They're all… unique. Olivia's so sharp, and Riley's got that attitude, and then there's Emma…"

Jessica's smile widened, a genuine, almost nostalgic warmth spreading across her face. "I think… I'd have to say Emma." Alissa blinked, a little surprised. Emma was certainly devoted to Junior, almost to a fault, but she'd also been through so much. "Emma?" she asked, her brow furrowed slightly. "Really? Why her?"

"Because," Jessica explained, leaning forward slightly, "her desire for Junior is just so raw and unfiltered. It's like you can see it churning inside her, this absolute need that shines through everything she does. It reminds me so much of my own… well, of Jennifer, when she was younger. That same intense, all-consuming devotion. It's captivating, in a way. It's like watching someone who's found their absolute center, their purpose, and it's just… him. And Junior, he really does bring out the best in her, doesn't he? He's her rock, her anchor, and she's just so… grateful for him."

Jessica's gaze softened as she spoke about Emma's devotion, a wistful, almost melancholic quality creeping into her voice. Suddenly, the playful spark in her eyes seemed to deepen, taking on a different hue. "It's a beautiful thing, that kind of absolute surrender," Jessica continued, her voice a little breathier now. "When someone's entire world revolves around another, not out of obligation, but out of pure, unadulterated love. And the way Emma looks at Junior… it's like he hung the moon and stars. It's a level of adoration that's truly… arresting."

Alissa took a sip of water, considering Jessica's words. "It's definitely… intense. I just worry sometimes. You know, Emma's been through so much. I hope this 'high protocol submissive training' isn't pushing her too far." Jessica chuckled. "Oh, honey, you're thinking like an engineer's wife. Everything's about pressure points and structural integrity.

This isn't about breaking Emma. It's about…" she paused, searching for the right words, "…synchronizing the satellites. Junior suddenly has three wives, almost all at once, all orbiting him at the same time. He needs them on the same page, or things are going to get… messy. Think of it as relationship firmware update."

"Synchronizing the satellites… relationship firmware update… Jessica, sometimes I swear you speak a different language. A language of… well, frankly, it sounds like something out of a very interesting adult film." Alissa said, setting Tyler on the ground. Jessica threw her head back and laughed, a rich, throaty sound that filled the room. "Oh, darling Alissa, you wound me! I'm merely applying a bit of… colorful analogy to a complex situation. Think of it this way: Junior loves these women, but he's also a leader, a protector. He needs to ensure their safety, not just physically, but emotionally. And in this… unique situation, well, traditional relationship counseling just isn't going to cut it."

"But high protocol submissive training? It sounds… controlling. Isn't that the opposite of love?" Alissa asked, her brow furrowed with genuine concern. "I mean, I love Aidan, but I wouldn't want him dictating my every move. That sounds more like… ownership." Jessica leaned forward, her voice lowering. "Ownership is a very loaded term, Alissa. There's a world of difference between healthy dominance and abusive control. What Junior's doing… it's more about establishing clear boundaries, understanding desires, and creating a safe space for these women to explore their own submission. Especially Emma."

Alissa digested her words, swirling the water in her glass. "It's just… Emma's been through so much. Davis… what he did… it's horrific. I worry that all this… BDSM stuff… it's just another form of trauma. Another way to be controlled." Jessica's softened her gaze, a hint of sadness entering her voice. "You see, Alissa, that's where you're wrong. It can be exactly the opposite." Jessica repositioned her feet, as if preparing to deliver a lecture. "Imagine Emma, imagining that same horrific incident, over and over again. If Junior does the same thing, the person, the act, even the intent becomes something positive, not negative. The key word is consent. No one is forcing Emma, or Olivia or Riley, to do anything they don't want to do. This is about them reclaiming their power, controlling their own narrative, even in the bedroom."

Taylor, who had been silently observing, chimed in. "It's a bit like Basic Training, you know? You don't go through it your whole career, but it instills a discipline, a way of thinking. You can always spot someone who's been through it, even years later." "Exactly!" Jessica snapped her fingers. "Protocol training creates a mindset, it conditions their understanding, and sets the groundwork for a functional power dynamic. It's not about obedience, it's about communication, trust, and… well, let's just say it can be incredibly liberating."

Suddenly, a thought struck Alissa. "So, what happens when they… graduate? From protocol training, I mean. Do they get a certificate? A party? Is there like, a submissive graduation ceremony?" "A submissive graduation ceremony?" Jessica squealed, her eyes sparkling with mischievous delight as she clapped her hands together. "Oh, Alissa, you brilliant girl! That would be simply divine! Imagine, a graduation ceremony, with speeches, awards... maybe a ceremonial collar presentation!"

Taylor leaned back on the plush sofa. "David would have hated it. Too much fuss and fanfare. He prefers... subtle displays of affection." "Subtle is an understatement," Jessica countered, playfully rolling her eyes. "David's a soft Dom. More like a benevolent dictator handing out back scratches and philosophical musings."

Alissa chuckled. "So, no protocol training for David's wives?" Jessica shook her head. "Nope. Too much effort. Besides, we all came in staggered, remember? There was already an orbit established. We all just sort of... slotted in." "Like a well-oiled machine," Taylor added with a wry smile. "A very happy well-oiled machine," Jessica corrected, nudging Taylor with her elbow. "Besides, David's not exactly the type to hand out homework assignments. He's more of a 'tell me your woes and I'll solve them with a cup of tea and a gentle head pat' kind of dominant."

Alissa considered this. "So, what exactly is protocol training? You mentioned collars?" Jessica's face grew serious. "Well, there are different levels. Some High Protocol dominants will award the 'Slave Collar', which is basically the black belt of high protocol submission." Alissa's eyes widened. "A slave collar? Isn't that... extreme?" "It's symbolic, Alissa!" Jessica said quickly, her tone defensive. "It's about owning your submission, not being owned. It's a sign of dedication, trust, and a deep understanding of the dynamic."

Taylor chimed in, "Think of it like a wedding ring. It's a piece of jewelry that signifies commitment and belonging, but it doesn't mean you lose your autonomy." "Okay," Alissa said slowly, still feeling a little bewildered. "So, what does this training actually involve?" Jessica launched into a detailed explanation, outlining the various stages, from learning basic etiquette and communication protocols to exploring personal limits and desires. She spoke of safe words, aftercare, and the importance of open and honest communication.

As Jessica spoke, Alissa couldn't help but think of Aidan. He was a mechanic, an engineer. He built things, fixed things. The idea of him leading a submissive training program seemed… absurd. "So, you're saying that Junior is basically running a BDSM finishing school?" Alissa asked, trying to lighten the mood.

Jessica threw her head back and laughed again. "You could say that! Except, instead of learning how to curtsy and pour tea, they're learning how to… well, you know." Just then, David walked into the living room, a stack of books in his arms. "What's all this talk about finishing schools?" he asked, his eyes twinkling. "Planning a field trip?" "We were just discussing Junior's… extracurricular activities," Taylor said with a sly smile.

David raised an eyebrow. "Ah, yes. The Dominant-in-Training. How's he progressing?" "Apparently, he's awarding slave collars," Alissa said, unable to resist the urge to see David's reaction. David chuckled. "If Junior's girls knew there was a 'Submissive Supreme' title up for grabs, complete with official collar, Junior would have to start rationing the safe words." He paused, stroking his chin thoughtfully. "A submissive earning a slave collar from her master is like a Soldier earning a Legion of Merit. It's a hard-earned privilege and a source of great pride, especially from someone as well-respected as Junior."

Jessica sighed dramatically, leaning back against the plush sofa. "Honestly, sometimes I wish you awarded slave collars, Daddy." She batted her eyelashes at him, a playful look in her eyes. "Imagine the bragging rights." Tiffany, who had been quietly observing the conversation, snorted. "Bragging rights? Jessica, we're not in some reality TV show. We're trying to rebuild civilization, remember?" "And what better way to rebuild civilization than with a clearly defined hierarchy of domestic discipline?" Jessica retorted, her voice dripping with sarcasm.

"Speaking of collars," David said, "I happened to be down in the work shed yesterday and noticed something rather… interesting. Seems Kyle has taken a particular interest in metalworking lately." Jessica's eyes widened. "Oh? What kind of metalworking?" David leaned in conspiratorially. "Let's just say it involves shaping metal into… neckwear. And, from what I could tell, they weren't for the cows."

Jessica gasped. "Slave collars! He's making slave collars for Junior, isn't he?" Tiffany widened her eyes. "Seriously?" "Hey, if the girls want to play 'Fifty Shades of Central Texas,' who are we to judge?" Taylor said, stifling a giggle. "I'm simply pointing out," David said, a slight smirk playing on his lips, "that Junior's symbolic standard of complete submission, involves solid metal collars, just like the one Jennifer wears." He paused, looking pointedly at Jennifer.

Jennifer beamed, stroking the smooth metal of the collar around her neck. "He was inspired by my eternity collar? I guess that's how he came up with the idea," she said proudly. "It is a rather fetching design, if I do say so myself!"

Meanwhile, on the other side of the ridge, a very different scene was unfolding. Seth and Noah, fresh from their hilltop sniper escapade, approached the five individuals Noah had so efficiently dispatched. Noah seemed particularly pleased with himself, though Seth wasn't as impressed. "Seriously, Noah?" Seth said, surveying the scene with a critical eye. "Four shots, five hits. Good, I guess. But look at the weaponry! Pathetic." He kicked at a rusty shotgun lying near one of the bodies. "A twenty-gauge? I haven't seen one of these since I was ten. And that pistol…" He wrinkled his nose. "I wouldn't use that for target practice."

Noah, beaming, puffed out his chest a little. "Hey, I got the job done, didn't I? Besides, what do you expect out here? It's not like we're fighting Navy SEALs." He bent down, rummaging through the debris. "Hold on, though... these might be useful." He emerged, brandishing a couple of cheap AR-15s and a well-worn Savage .223. "ARs are a dime a dozen, but they still go for something. And the .223 is a decent enough varmint gun. We can use these for bartering, right? "

Seth grudgingly conceded. "Yeah, I guess so. We can probably hand them off to some unfortunate survivalists." He sighed dramatically. "The collapse of civilization really did a number on the quality of firearms, didn't it?" Noah, still meticulously examining the bodies, suddenly stopped. "Huh. That's a relief." Noah declared, his shoulders visibly slumping.

Seth, mid-kick at another mangled weapon, paused, one eyebrow arched higher than the other. "A relief? What, you thought they were gonna jump back up and ask for autographs?" He turned to face Noah, shovel leaning casually against his shoulder. "Or did you finally realize killing people, even the not-so-bright ones, isn't as fun as popping tin cans?" Noah shook his head, relief still washing over him. "No, man." He gestured vaguely at the bodies. "They're not... they're not thick Latinas."

Seth blinked. Then he burst out laughing, a hearty, booming sound that echoed across the hillside. "You're serious? You're actually relieved that the guys you just sniped aren't fulfilling your... specific... criteria?" He wiped a tear from his eye. "Only you, Noah. Only you could turn a post-apocalyptic firefight into a freaking dating app filter!"

He straightened up, still chuckling. "Alright, alright. Enough goofing off. Let's get these guys buried before the buzzards start sending in Yelp reviews. You grab the shovels, I'll... uh... check for any hidden treasure." "Speaking of... dating... how's our little Bonnie doing?" Noah asked, grabbing the shovels.

Seth's humming stopped abruptly. "Bonnie's…" he hesitated, then sighed. "She's… curious. You know she's been watching David's wives and is trying to learn how to be a woman." "You know, Bonnie's not the only one who's been watching those women," Noah said, driving his shovel into the dirt. "I've been paying attention too." Seth raised an eyebrow. "Oh? And what have you learned?"

Noah shrugged. "I've learned that there's more to being a man than just being strong and skilled with a gun. There's a certain... gentleness that I've seen in some of the husbands here. A willingness to listen and care for their wives, even when they're in the middle of a crisis."

Seth was surprised by Noah's observation. It was true that the men in their community had a unique balance of strength and compassion, something that had become increasingly rare in the world before the apocalypse. "I think that's what Bonnie is looking for," Noah continued. "She wants to know what it means to be a woman, but she also wants to know what it means to be loved and cherished by a man who truly cares for her."

Seth nodded, understanding dawning on him. "So, she's not just looking for a collar. She's looking for someone who will treat her with respect and kindness, even in the midst of chaos." Noah smiled. "Exactly. And I think that's something we can all learn from, don't you?" He leaned on his shovel again, a thoughtful expression on his face. "Besides, who needs a collar when you've got a diamond ring?" He couldn't help but add the joke.

Seth chuckled and then said, "Speaking of which, I told Bonnie she can wear a choker if it makes her feel 'claimed' but she can only wear a collar if I can marry multiple women." Noah tilted his head. "And how did Miss Bonnie take that offer?" Seth sighed dramatically and said, "She prefers her diamond ring, one woman only, and she hasn't brought it up since." He rolled his eyes playfully. "I think she was just trying to see how far she could push me. She's got a mischievous streak a mile wide, that one." Noah laughed. "Just make sure you're thinking about that when she starts asking for a pony and a solid gold swing set for her birthday."

Chapter 5:

The Collaring Ceremony

David stood at the top of the porch, his presence commanding without being overtly theatrical. His eyes swept over the faces of his extended family; his wives, his children, his sons and daughters-in-law, and the many others who had found refuge and purpose within these walls. Jennifer, his second wife, stood beside him. She was captivating even in the subdued light, her eyes fixed on David. Tiffany, Elena, Jessica, Summer, Nicole, Taylor, Kayla, and Tanya were all present, each a testament to David's unique capacity for leadership and connection.

David Junior stood a few paces away, his typical intensity softened by an undercurrent of anticipation. Beside him, Emma, Olivia, and Riley were poised, their expressions a blend of solemnity and quiet resolve. They each wore a beautiful dress, their hair neatly restrained, every line of their bodies communicating a disciplined readiness. The three months had visibly molded them, not just physically, but in the aura they projected, a quiet strength that transcended mere physical prowess.

David let the silence stretch for a moment longer, allowing the gravity of the moment to settle upon everyone present. Then, his voice, clear and resonant, filled the space. "We gather here this evening for a deeply significant occasion," David began, his gaze briefly resting on Junior, then on the three women. "Three months ago, Emma, Olivia, and Riley embarked on a challenging, deeply personal journey. A journey of self-discovery, of unwavering commitment, and of profound trust. They began their high-protocol submissive training, and today, they stand before us having completed every single rigorous requirement."

A low murmur of appreciation rippled through the gathering. Aidan, standing with Alissa, nodded subtly, understanding the depth of dedication such training demanded. Brian, his hand resting gently on Seo-Yeon shifted, his expression respectful. Josh, ever vigilant, stood near Lily, who watched with a fierce admiration in her eyes. The younger members, Seth, Grace, and even Poppy, watched with an understandable curiosity, though the full weight of the ceremony was perhaps yet to be truly felt by them.

David paused again, allowing his words to hang in the air. "This was not an easy path. They have spent these past ninety days perfecting submissive positions that speak of absolute trust and surrender. They have endured exhaustive endurance training and testing, pushing past limits they once thought insurmountable. They have learned to push their bodies and minds beyond preconceived boundaries, to find strength in vulnerability, and to build an unshakeable foundation of resilience."

He moved his hand in a subtle, encompassing gesture towards his wives. "More than that, they have spent countless hours learning every skill, every nuanced understanding, taught by each of my own wives; women who embody strength, loyalty, and the deepest forms of partnership.

His gaze returned to Emma, Olivia, and Riley, a profound respect in his eyes. "But perhaps most importantly, each and every day, Emma, Olivia, and Riley have proven their unwavering commitment to Junior. They have shown a dedication that is truly inspiring, a resolve that speaks volumes about the depth of their love and the strength of their character. In a world where so much is uncertain, where the very ground beneath us shifted just over a year ago, their commitment to building a strong, unified family with Junior is a beacon. It is a light that cuts through the darkness, illuminating the path forward for all of us."

The air seemed to crackle with the intensity of his words. There was no pretense, no flattery, only unvarnished truth. This was not about subjugation, but about the consensual, profound forging of bonds in a harsh new reality. "Through their perseverance, their discipline, and their deep-seated desire to honor Junior and this shared life, they have earned a profound honor. They have earned the right to wear the ultimate symbol of their devotion and their place within our family: their own eternity collars."

David's voice deepened, taking on a more protective, almost guttural quality. "Let there be no misunderstanding. These collars do not represent weakness. They represent absolute strength. They are not a mark of subjugation, but a declaration of resolve, a testament to an unshakeable bond freely chosen and fiercely protected. They are a visible testament to the profound trust and commitment exchanged between Junior and these women. And let this be known to all, now and forever: these collars serve as a sacred vow, a promise whispered in the heart of this family."

He paused, his voice dropping slightly, the intensity in his eyes sharpening. "And they also serve as an immutable warning. A public declaration of the ultimate protection afforded to these women. Anyone, anyone, who dares to lay a harmful hand upon a woman wearing one of these collars, anyone who seeks to diminish, to disrespect, or to inflict pain upon Emma, Olivia, or Riley, will face the absolute torment of every soul under this roof. We are family, bound by blood, by choice, and by the unforgiving lessons of this new world. And we protect our own with a ferocity that knows no bounds. These collars are not just symbols; they are a shield, forged in trust and backed by every ounce of our collective might."

A collective shiver ran through the crowd, not of fear, but of grim understanding and unwavering solidarity. Darrel stood straighter, his hand instinctively going to Reagan's. Caleb and Sophia exchanged a look of understanding. Even the night shift crew, Andrew, Susan, Noah, Kathy, and Callie, who had arrived just before the ceremony, absorbed David's chilling promise with silent assent.

In the quiet that followed, Kyle stepped forward from the small group near David, holding a dark velvet tray. Three shining collars gleamed in the subdued light, elegantly simple yet undeniably weighty with meaning. Each was a perfect, unbroken circle, a symbol of eternity. Kyle handled them with a surprising gentleness as he presented them to Junior.

Junior took the first collar, his movements precise and deliberate. He approached Emma, his eyes meeting hers, a silent exchange passing between them. With perfect precision, Emma moved, kneeling gracefully before him, her head bowed in a posture of complete trust and reverence. She remained still, her breath even, as Junior carefully fastened the collar around her neck. The click of the clasp was audible in the hushed room, a definitive sound sealing a sacred pact.

Next, Junior turned to Olivia. She, too, moved with an almost ethereal grace, sinking to her knees, her dark hair falling forward as she bowed her head. Junior's hands were steady, his gaze unwavering as he placed the second collar. Olivia's intelligence, a quality that had drawn her to Junior, now shone in the quiet dignity of her submission.

Finally, Riley approached. There was no trace of her usual playful defiance now, only a serene composure. She knelt with the same fluid motion, her posture one of quiet strength. Junior leaned in, his expression tender and possessive, as he secured the final collar around her neck. The silver gleamed against her skin, a stark contrast, yet a perfect fit.

The three women remained kneeling, their positions perfect, a living tableau of absolute trust and surrender. The collars, far from being chains, seemed to radiate a silent power around them. They were not just adornments but declarations, etched in silver and sworn in the presence of their family. David's voice, rich and resonant, broke the silence. "Emma, Olivia, Riley," he began, his gaze sweeping over each woman, then to Junior. "Stand now, and join your husband."

A collective sigh of relief, light as a whisper, rippled through the assembled crowd. Emma, Olivia, and Riley rose, their movements still graceful, but imbued now with a lightness, a joyous lifting of spirits. Pride swelled within them, an elation that was palpable. They turned and moved, almost in unison, to stand beside Junior, who extended a hand to each, drawing them close into a protective arc, a subtle but unmistakable claiming.

Emma, ever practical and curious, leaned in, her voice a low whisper that only Junior could hear. "What are these made of?" she murmured, her fingers tracing the smooth, cool metal of the collar. It felt substantial, weighty, unlike anything she'd ever encountered. Junior's lips curved into a small, pleased smile. "Titanium," he whispered back, his thumb rubbing lightly over the metal. "With solid 24-carat gold cores." He paused, a hint of his characteristic swagger returning. "Figured if you're gonna commit, it might as well be to something that'll outlast the apocalypse, and look damned good doing it."

Olivia, usually the quietest, let out a soft, surprised gasp, her eyes widening as she touched her own collar. "Gold?" she echoed, a faint blush rising on her cheeks. "Junior, how did you even...?" "Five ounces. Pure, 24-carat gold. Each," he declared, his voice low enough to remain a whisper. "Melted down from my own bullion stash. Figured if I was going to lock you three down, it needed to be with something as precious as you are."

Olivia gasped again, a more pronounced sound this time. Her hand flew to her mouth. "Five ounces?! Junior, that's... that's an insane amount of gold! You could buy... well, a lot of chickens, I guess, in this economy." Her cheeks were now decidedly pink, a stark contrast to the gleaming collar. Emma tilted her head, her gaze thoughtful. "But seriously, where did you stash enough bullion for fifteen ounces of 24-carat gold? I thought we were all living off the land and repurposed scrap metal."

Junior chuckled. "You think David just built this fortress and stocked it with canned goods and bullets? My dad's been stockpiling bullion since we were children, waiting for the inevitable. He's got enough to restart a small economy, probably. The man thinks twenty-five years ahead, minimum. And hey," he winked, "I learned from the best. I've got my own little safety net, a share of the family fortune, so to speak.

David, watching the tender moment with a knowing smile, cleared his throat, his voice resonating across the quiet gathering. "By the power vested in me by... well, by the sheer necessity of surviving an apocalypse and building a new society," he declared with a twinkle in his eye, "I now pronounce you, husband and wives."

A smattering of applause and warm murmurs filled the air as David concluded the ceremony, a sense of quiet joy settling over the family. As the crowd began to stir, ready to transition from ceremony to celebration, a different kind of energy began to build on the porch. Brian, Aidan, Seth, Lily, and Grace, who had been quietly congregating near a makeshift stage setup earlier in the day, began to move with purpose. The air practically hummed with anticipation, a lighthearted counterpoint to the gravitas of the ceremony.

The entire crowd of extended family members and community members watched with a mixture of curiosity and confusion. Emma, still processing the moment, leaned into Junior. "Are they... about to put on a play?" Junior grinned, a mischievous glint in his eyes. "Better. Much, much better."

Aidan, looking every inch the rock god in waiting, unslung a gleaming electric guitar from its stand, its polished surface catching the fading sunlight. He then flashed a blinding smile at Alissa, who stood by with a playful eye-roll and a proud smirk. "Alright, alright, check one, two!" he called out, tapping the microphone attached to the stand.

Grace, meanwhile, was already seated behind a drum kit that looked surprisingly professional. Her usually sweet face was set in an expression of intense focus, her sticks twirling with surprising dexterity. She caught Kyle's eye, who was standing a little awkwardly, trying to look cool but clearly flustered as she gave him a triumphant, almost possessive nod.

Lily, a picture of effortless cool, slung her white bass guitar over her shoulder. Josh just stood near the front, arms crossed, a proud, almost proprietary smile playing on his lips. Seth, looking earnest and a little overwhelmed but completely determined, took Junior's guitar, a Gibson ES-335. He glanced over at Bonnie, who was practically vibrating with excitement in the audience, and tried to affect a cool, nonchalant pose that mostly came off as adorable.

Finally, Brian stepped up to the microphone, adjusting it to accommodate his towering height as he leaned into his synth touchpad. The newer arrivals, a significant portion of the audience, exchanged bewildered glances. Andrew nudged Susan, whispering, "Did they... did they just pull a full band out of nowhere?" Susan, ever kind, just shrugged, a small smile forming. "Looks like it. I didn't know anyone here played."

Darrel, witty and observant, tugging at Reagan's hand. "Well, bless our apocalypse-addled hearts, I think we're about to get a concert." Reagan chuckled. "A concert? Out here? I swear, this family is always full of surprises." David, however, watching from his prime spot next to Tiffany and Jessica, simply smiled, a deep, contented look on his face.

His wives clustered around him, each with a knowing, nostalgic glint in their eyes. Tiffany beamed with maternal pride. "Oh, this is going to be good," she murmured, a hand on his arm. "They haven't done this since Jessica's wedding." Jessica, leaning into David's side, patted his leg playfully. "Daddy, look at them. They're all grown up and still rocking out."

The first chords ripped through the air, heavy and unmistakable. A driving, powerful riff from Aidan's guitar, met by a thunderous, precise beat from Grace. Lily laid down a deep, resonant bassline that seemed to vibrate the very ground beneath them. Brian's synth added layers of atmospheric sound, creating a surprisingly full and professional wall of noise. Seth joined in with a soaring melody line, still trying to look cool for Bonnie.

It was Boston's "Don't Look Back," and Aidan's voice, surprisingly strong and clear, poured over the crowd. He wasn't just singing; he was performing, swaying with the music, his hair falling into his eyes, his entire being radiating the joy of it. Alissa had to bite back a laugh, but her eyes held undeniable adoration. She bounced baby Tyler gently in her arms, who seemed surprisingly placid, perhaps lulled by the vibrations.

The newer arrivals, initially stunned, started to tap their feet. Andrew and Susan exchanged wide-eyed grins. Caleb, usually reserved, bobbed his head slightly, Sophia leaning into him with a quiet smile. Kathy, the realist, had a look of genuine astonishment. "Well, I'll be," she muttered, "Who knew this place came with rock stars?"

Darrel leaned over to Reagan. "See? I told you this place was more than just a fortified bunker of ingenuity. It's also… a fortified bunker of rock and roll." Reagan smacked his arm playfully, laughing. Jennifer, leaning against David's side, murmured, "They're good, Master. Really good." He squeezed her hand affectionately. Jessica, holding little Poppy, swayed gently. "Daddy, think they know AC/DC?" she stage-whispered, a mischievous glint in her eye.

The crowd in front of the house began to quiet as the band built toward the crescendo, halfway through the song. Aidan's fingers, a blur across the fretboard, tapped the guitar with a fervor that was both precise and wildly uninhibited. His riffs, sharp and soaring, began to climb, echoing the rising tension in the melody. Beside him, Seth, his eyes closed in concentration, added a layer of rhythmic chorus repeats, each one gaining a little more urgency, a little more volume. Behind them, Grace was a drumming prodigy. Her hands were a whirlwind of motion, her stickwork on the high hats a rolling, incessant rhythm that pulled the entire soundscape upwards, an invisible rope tugging on the very air.

The energy in the valley was palpable, a buzzing, vibrating current that seeped into everyone's bones. Brian, at the synth, was no longer just providing backing; he was adding shimmering, ethereal layers that somehow made the rock even more massive, his body subtly swaying in time with Grace's accelerating tempo.

Then came Grace's drumroll. An undeniably motivating sequence that didn't just build momentum, it demanded attention, a percussive announcement that something truly spectacular was about to happen. It was a visceral, heart-thumping warning, pushing the rhythm guitar higher and higher. It wasn't just a sound; it was a physical force. Bone-chilling, as Jessica had noted, but also exhilarating.

The ground beneath everyone's feet seemed to hum, the vibrations travelling straight up their legs, through their chests, making teeth subtly chatter. Her fingers danced with a terrifying grace, pulling forth notes that resonated in chests, making the very air thick with the deep, resonant rumble. Lily's bass, along with Grace's crashing cymbals and Aidan's unrestrained jamming, crashed all at once. It wasn't just loud; it was an immersive experience, a wave of pure sound that seemed to nearly blow everyone away, sweeping through the crowd like a joyful, controlled explosion.

As the final, ringing note faded into the evening air, a deafening cheer erupted from the crowd. People clapped, stomped, and whistled, their faces flushed with exhilaration. Aiden, grinning wildly, threw his arms up, his chest heaving after the intense performance. Grace collapsed onto her drum stool, giggling, as Seth offered a high-five, and Brian gave a thumbs-up.

Suddenly, a new figure stepped onto the makeshift stage. Junior moved with a confident stride. He approached Seth, who was still basking in the applause, and with a quick, understanding nod, took back his guitar. Seth, without missing a beat, smoothly transitioned to the drum kit, sliding onto Grace's stool as she vacated it. Then, to everyone's slight surprise, David walked up and took Lily's bass, adjusting the strap with a calm, practiced air that no one knew he possessed. Lily just smirked and gave him a playful shove, clearly inviting him to show what he had.

Aidan, Brian, and Grace, still buzzing, exchanged amused glances before joining the audience. Alissa immediately wrapped Aidan in a hug, murmuring her praise. "You were incredible!" she whispered, pressing a kiss to his damp temple. Tiffany, his mother, clapped him on the back.

"Alright, folks!" Junior's voice, amplified through the modest system, cut through the residual cheers. He strummed a few familiar chords, a grin spreading across his face. "Hope you're ready for more! We're gonna keep the party going!" Aidan settled next to Alissa, leaning into her embrace. "Think they can top that?" he whispered, a playful challenge in his tone. Alissa chuckled. "Darling, with Junior on guitar and

David on bass? Anything is possible. Though I admit, David's choice of instrument is... unexpected."

Just then, David nodded subtly at Junior and Seth. The first, unmistakable notes of "Cliffs of Dover" sliced through the cool evening air. Junior's fingers danced across the fretboard, each note precise, ringing with an almost impossible clarity. It wasn't just fast; it was clean, every bend, every hammer-on, every pull-off executed with surgical accuracy. The crowd, initially cheering for the new lineup, quickly fell into a stunned silence.

The final echoing note of "Cliffs of Dover" faded, and Alissa, nestled beside Aidan blinked, genuinely stunned. She'd known David's family was... talented. But this? Alissa squeezed Aidan's hand, a silent question passing between them. Was this level of skill even fair? He chuckled quietly, shaking his head. "They're good at pretty much everything. Makes you wonder what they're not good at, doesn't it?"

Across the yard, Andrew, Susan clinging to his arm, nursed a simmering resentment. It wasn't just astonishment; it was a weird, unsettling feeling of...betrayal? He strummed his guitar every night, dreaming of being a rock star. He'd even told Junior about his aspirations a few times, and Junior had just nodded politely. Now, seeing him shred like that... it felt like a personal affront. "Show off," he muttered under his breath.

"Show off," Andrew grumbled, the words barely audible to Susan, who immediately elbowed him playfully. "Maybe he was being humble? Or maybe... maybe this is an opportunity! You can start a band! You know, with him! You guys could be awesome!" She punctuated her suggestion with an encouraging squeeze of his arm. Andrew hesitated. The idea was actually... appealing. Imagining himself on stage with Junior, shredding solos alongside him, was a lot more palatable than just simmering in resentment. "Besides," Susan added, tilting her head towards the makeshift stage, "the secret's out now. And look at Olivia, Riley, and Emma. They're practically glowing with pride. You know how much Junior loves to make people happy."

Andrew followed her gaze. Olivia, Riley, and Emma were indeed beaming, their faces radiant. They huddled around Junior, bombarding him with questions and showering him with praise. The titanium collars, gleaming in the fading light, seemed to amplify their joy. "I had no idea you could even hold a guitar, let alone play like that!" Olivia exclaimed, her voice bubbling with enthusiasm. Riley simply said, "Damn, Junior. You were holding out on us! That was hotter than hell."

The shift in instruments was as sudden as it was comical. Andrew gawked, mouth agape, as David hopped onto the drum kit. Brian, who had just returned to the porch, was now cradling Lily's bass. Lily, not missing a beat, snatched Aidan's guitar, and Grace made off with Junior's beloved axe. "What the fuck!" Andrew blurted out, forgetting his earlier attempt at cool resentment. Susan, startled, grabbed his arm. "What is it?"

"Did you see that? It's like...musical chairs, but with, like, actual musicians!" He gestured wildly at the impromptu stage. "He just watched several members of David's family jump from one instrument to the next like musical chairs" Before Susan could even process the spectacle, David and Grace, with an almost telepathic understanding, launched into the opening riffs of "Sultans of Swing." The music was tight, clean, and undeniably…good. Andrew stood frozen, his brain struggling to reconcile what he was seeing with his preconceived notions of…well, everything.

He turned to Junior, who was still basking in the glow of his wives' adoration. "Dude…how many instruments can you guys even play?" Junior chuckled. "It's kind of a family thing. We got some basics from dad. Drums, bass, and trumpet – everyone in the family can handle those. Aidan, Brian, Lily, Seth, Grace, and I all learned the guitar. Brian, Lily, Tiffany, Aidan, and Jessica are pretty decent on the piano. And Summer? I think she use to play the clarinet."

The aroma of barbeque, mingled with potatoes and toppings wafted through the air, carrying on the gentle breeze. The main stage had become a free for all where even Parker and Andrew got to show their talents, even if just a bit. The crowd, fueled by barbeque and camaraderie, was a mix of ages and personalities, spread from the back deck of the main house, flowing onto the wrap-around porch, and spilling into the yard.

While Parker was trying to impress his wife with his rendition of his favorite country song, Jill was currently more interested in critiquing Scott's grilling technique. "Scott," Jill called out, her voice carrying over the music, "are you sure you seasoned that right? It smells suspiciously like…meat." Scott, spatula in hand, turned, a look of mock offense on his face. "Jill, I'll have you know, I'm the butcher! And I invented meat! And this," he gestured dramatically with the spatula, "is a culinary masterpiece!"

As the evening wore on, the party started to wind down. The kids were getting sleepy, even Tyler, who'd been remarkably well-behaved all evening. As the clock approached 10:00 PM, David clapped his hands, drawing everyone's attention. "Alright, everyone! Time to call it a night! I think it's time for Junior to take his wives back to the apartment and enjoy their night, I'll cover his night shift"

Junior, a lazy grin spreading across his face, wrapped his arms around Emma, Olivia, and Riley. "Sounds good to me. Thanks, Dad." He looked at Andrew and Susan. "See you two around." With a chorus of goodnights and the night shift starting the cleanup, the crowd began to disperse. David lingered with Andrew and Susan, watching as Junior led his wives towards the work shed.

"So," David said, turning to Andrew with a knowing smile, "I hear you're wondering about the whole 'musical family' thing." Andrew nodded, still a little dazed. "Yeah, just a bit. How did it all happen?" David chuckled. "Well, let's just say I've had a little help. Remember how I lived through this life once before?" Andrew's eyes widened. "Yeah…"

"Well," David continued, leaning in, "in that life, I learned to play the trumpet when I was in school. The bass I picked up later, for Jessica. I wanted to play it for her. And the drums? That was for the kids. I wanted them to have something fun to do. When I regressed, those skills, for some reason, became permanent. It's like my brain was hardwired with the knowledge."

He paused, noticing Andrew's dumbfounded expression. "And as for the kids…well, they inherited the musical gene, let's say. They learned the rest themselves, growing up. They all have a knack for it." Andrew stared at David, his mind still struggling to process everything. "So, basically, you're saying you're a time-traveling, musically gifted…" "Patriarch?" David finished, a grin spreading across his face. "Something like that. Don't worry, it didn't all come naturally. They all practiced hard!"

David smiled before continuing. "It's easy to learn new things when you already have a head start. I told y'all before, if there's something you want to learn, just ask. Someone here can probably help you." Andrew's eyes darted around the receding crowd, now suddenly noticing the array of skills and knowledge concentrated within the ranch. He'd been so focused on surviving and finding his place that he hadn't truly appreciated the goldmine of learning opportunities surrounding him.

Susan nudged him gently. "He's right, you know. You were always talking about wanting to learn guitar. Plus, I heard the children practice knife juggling." A flush crept up Andrew's neck. Everyone always seemed to offer an opportunity to learn. He'd dismissed the offer, too caught up in feeling inadequate. But now, seeing the ease with which Seth and Aidan shredded on their guitars, a spark of envy, and a desire to learn, ignited within him. "I… I should have,"

Andrew mumbled, kicking at a loose stone. "I just didn't want to be a burden, you know? Everyone's so busy."

"Nonsense, Andrew," David said, clapping him on the shoulder, "It's never too late to learn something new. And as for being a burden? This is a community, son. We help each other. Where else are you gonna find a better mix of skills in such a permissive environment? Here, you're surrounded by potential. You just have to reach out and grab it." David winked, then scanned the room. "Plus, I've been meaning to start a music class. The more the merrier!" Susan beamed at Andrew, squeezing his hand. "See? No excuses now!"

Just then, Brian, his face alight with a rare smile, approached them. "Hey, Andrew," he said, his voice surprisingly enthusiastic. "I overheard what David was saying. I'd be happy to work with you on the guitar. I haven't had much chance to play lately, and honestly, it's not like I have to watch my plants grow. They mostly just, uh, grow." He shrugged. "Besides," he added, glancing at the guitars leaning against the wall, "it'd be good to have someone to jam with who isn't Seo-Yeon. All she likes is K-Pop, and I don't have the heart to explain the superiority of Metallica to her."

Andrew chuckled, relief washing over him. "Seriously? You'd do that? I mean, you're always so…busy." Brian waved a dismissive hand. "Busy is relative. I keep myself busy, but the garden's going to grow whether I'm there or not." "See, Andrew?" David chuckled. "Opportunity knocks."

Chapter 6:

The Mulcher's Discussion

Nestled in the Work Shed, the mulcher squatted like a hungry, metallic beast. Its primary diet this morning was the ranch's meticulously sorted garbage. This was not the refuse of a consumerist society, but the minimalist leavings of a truly off-grid, self-sufficient community. Yet, even minimal waste, when accumulated, demanded attention.

Mark braced himself against the mulcher's frame. He plunged another handful of flattened plastic wrappers and crumpled foil into its maw, then leaned into the hand crank. "Who knew," he grunted, veins popping in his neck, "that the apocalypse meant less fighting off raiders and more... advanced recycling?"

Beside him, Eric, looking perpetually on the verge of a sigh, fed a stream of empty cereal bags into the chute. "At least it's not actual garbage," he muttered, his voice muffled by the clatter. "Remember that smell from the old dumpsters? That was a performance art piece in itself." Marvin pushed a contractor bag open, holding it steady for the mulched refuse. "You guys are just nostalgic for the good old days of city filth, aren't you? I, for one, prefer the scent of... well, of slightly less organized decay." He took a deep breath, then winced. "Okay, maybe not that much less organized."

The mulcher, a beast originally designed to devour branches, now gnawed through plastic with a surprisingly similar, though less woody, whine. It was slow work, demanding consistent effort, a monotonous grind that served as an unwelcome backdrop to their early morning. The small pile of neatly baled 'waste' they'd started with seemed to mock their progress. "I swear," Mark said, pushing hard on the crank, his brow furrowed in concentration, "this thing could probably mulch a small car if you fed it enough coffee. We should get Aidan to rig up a pedal system. Or a hamster wheel. Junior's guys could power it."

Eric, who had been feeding empty cereal bags into the chute with the precise, weary movements of a man performing a sacred ritual, finally straightened up, letting out a long, drawn-out sigh that seemed to deflate him slightly. "Mark, you know good and well why it's a hand-crank. It's intentional." He gestured vaguely at the mulcher with a plastic wrapper. "David's… vision. It's about fitness. Cross-training. Core strength. The 'holistic' approach to post-apocalyptic waste management."

Marvin scoffed, wrestling the contractor bag open wider. "Holistic? I think 'sadistic' is closer to the truth. My core feels more like it's been hit by a truck than toned. And I'm only twenty. What's Clarence doing to stay in shape? Knitting himself a new set of abs?" A thud from the apartment bunker's main access tunnel announced the arrival of the early risers. Josh and Lily emerged, looking far too bright-eyed for 8 AM on a Friday, carrying a couple of empty buckets.

"Morning, gentlemen of the refuse arts!" Lily chirped, her cheerful tone rubbing against their grumbling like sandpaper. "Getting a good workout in?" "Peachy," Mark grunted, sweat beading on his forehead. "Just trying to develop the triceps of a Norse god, one juice box at a time." "And the spiritual fortitude of a monk," Eric added, pushing another empty carton with a determined sigh. "You see, it's not just about the biceps, Mark. It's about the mind. The quiet contemplation of a yogurt cup's final moments. The zen of shredded cardboard."

Marvin rolled his eyes, managing to finally crush a particularly stubborn plastic jug. "My mind is contemplating a triple cheeseburger. With extra fries. And a side of 'not manually breaking down every single piece of refuse produced by sixty people'." He tossed the flattened jug into the mulcher, watching it disappear with a satisfying crunch.

Josh chuckled, his hands tucked into his pockets. "Well, at least you're all getting your steps in." They complained, yes, but there was a deep satisfaction in the knowledge that they were contributing, that their efforts kept the ranch running. "Speaking of things getting done," Lily continued, placing her empty buckets neatly beside a stack of clean rags. "The night shift was busy last night. Junior gave me a quick rundown before he hit the hay."

Eric paused his mulching, genuinely interested. "Oh? Moving some serious dirt, were they?" "More than serious dirt," Josh confirmed, leaning against a workbench. "They cleared out the last month's worth of compacted compost and the shredded refuse that was processed. Brian was saying the soil in the new composting plot is looking fantastic. Junior had them digging deeper than usual, really prepping it for the next round of back filling."

Lily grinned. "Andrew and Susan, along with Caleb and Sophia, they were on cart duty, ferrying it all away from the perimeter. Emma, Kathy, Riley, Olivia, and Callie were doing the final burial, making sure everything was properly covered and camouflaged. Junior's got them working hard, even when it's pitch black." "Good. Keeps the perimeter clean," Eric nodded, resuming his task with renewed vigor.

Mark leaned on the mulcher, catching his breath. "What's the word from the usual intel drops? Any whispers from the outside? Anything about the big cities?" Josh sighed, shaking his head slightly. "It's getting worse, Mark. Houston's a mess. Lily and I were talking before we came down here – their reserve fuel supplies are critically low. They're rationing everything, even generator power. No new shipments coming in, obviously, and what reserves they had is just… dwindling."

"Same with Dallas, from what Junior heard and what the scouts picked up," Lily added, her cheerfulness fading into a more somber, almost grim, expression. "A lot of those downtown communities that initially organized, thinking they could just run on what was left in the grid… they're starting to fall apart."

"No active supply chains, no way to get new fuel, new parts," Aidan's voice cut in from the doorway of the work shed. "They relied too much on what was already there, didn't they? Didn't plan for zero input. Or for things breaking down beyond simple fixes." Alissa, looking refreshed and holding several mugs of what smelled like freshly brewed coffee, nodded solemnly. "I brought you guys some coffee and cookies."

"Exactly," Josh agreed. "They set up these 'community hubs,' tried to get things organized, but without a reliable, self-sustaining power source, it's all just... wishful thinking. No infrastructure to support it long-term. No way to repair critical equipment quickly, no way to keep water purification systems running reliably if they break down, no way to feed their growing populations without a continuous supply chain."

"That's the difference, isn't it?" Eric mused, his complaints about the mulcher momentarily forgotten. "Here, we've got our own experts. We're producing our own food, generating our own power, purifying our own water, even making our own ammo. We're not reliant on old, crumbling systems that were designed for a different world."

"And David's temporal knowledge," Alissa added softly. "He built this place to be an island. An ark, almost. The others... they built lifeboats from pieces of the sinking ship, expecting rescue that never came." "And now those lifeboats are running out of paddles and patching material," Lily concluded, her voice low. "It's grim out there. Truly grim. Junior said he even heard isolated reports of communities resorting to... more aggressive methods of resource acquisition. That's why there have been more raids."

Marvin shivered, despite the relative warmth and security inside the shed. "Glad we're here, then. Even if it means my abs are getting a 'holistic' beating from this contraption." He grunted as he finally managed to flatten a particularly stubborn plastic bottle that had resisted his efforts.

"You know," Mark said. "It's funny, all this talk about adaptation. I mean, sure, we've all had to adapt to living off-grid, learning new skills, getting used to the quiet nights without city lights. But it's also bled into… other areas of life." He paused, a wry smile playing on his lips, looking from Eric to Josh, then finally settling on Alissa. "Janet and I, for example. Never, in all our married years, have we had a more 'exciting' personal life."

Josh raised an eyebrow, a slow grin spreading across his face. Eric coughed, trying to suppress a chuckle, while Alissa's cheeks flushed a delicate pink. Mark, oblivious or perhaps deliberately ignoring the reactions, continued, warming to his theme. "I mean, being confined to this lovely, secure, but ultimately finite space… it brings people closer. And not just emotionally, you know? The sheer lack of external distractions, the constant reminder of… well, of fragility, I suppose. It makes you appreciate everything a whole lot more. Even the little things. Especially the little things." He shifted his weight, his gaze drifting to the ceiling, as if reliving some private, delightful memory. "Janet even brought up, half-joking, of course… about implementing a 'free use' policy."

Alissa's blush deepened, drawing a snort from Marvin, who was now expertly feeding bottles into the press. Eric's suppressed chuckle finally broke free, a loud bark of laughter that echoed in the shed. Josh leaned his head back and guffawed, clapping his hands together. "A 'free use' policy, you say?" Josh managed between laughs. "Janet? Our Janet? The one who meticulously grades every single… everything?"

"Hey!" Mark protested, though he was grinning broadly now, clearly enjoying the reactions. "She said it was a 'thought experiment' on societal norms under extreme pressure! Something about maximizing communal well-being and reducing stress through… open engagement." He winked. "Or maybe she just misses having a good time."

Lily pushed herself off the workbench. With a glint in her eyes, she looked directly at Mark. "Don't be shy, Mark. David does the same thing with his wives. They never know when it's coming." She shrugged, her expression completely deadpan, then added, "It keeps them on their toes." The shed fell silent for a beat, the only sounds the rhythmic thump-crunch of Marvin's press. Eric's laughter died in his throat, replaced by a half-choked gasp. Alissa stared at Lily, her eyes wide, a mixture of shock and dawning amusement crossing her face.

Marvin stopped pressing, his eyes darting between Lily and the others. "Wait. What? He just… surprises them?" "That's what I said, Marvin. David does the same thing with his wives. They never know when it's coming." Lily shrugged, as if discussing the weather. "It keeps them on their toes. Keeps things… interesting, I guess."

Mark, still trying to look indignant but failing miserably, let out a snort. "Lily, you're an instigator. David is a man of… method." "Oh, he has methods, alright," Lily countered, a flicker of mischief finally entering her eyes. "Just not the ones you're thinking of. More like the 'element of surprise' method."

Josh looked up, a wry grin spreading across his face. "Well, come on, Marvin, think about it." He gestured. "David's got nine wives. It's not like he can have them all waiting in line outside his room, tapping their feet and asking for a numbered ticket. That'd be a logistical nightmare, not to mention a romance killer." Marvin blinked, a new layer of confusion settling on his features. "Nine wives… right. But, still. Anywhere?"

"Anywhere. Any time. Fair game," Josh confirmed, nodding. "It's why a lot of them lean towards dresses, you know. Easier access." He didn't elaborate, but the implication hung heavy in the air, eliciting a chorus of choking sounds from Eric and a sudden, loud cough from Mark, his shoulders shaking with silent laughter.

"Dresses for easier access…" Marvin repeated slowly, his mind clearly trying to compute this new-found information about the inner workings of David's sprawling marital bliss. "So… he just… goes for it? Whenever he feels like it? Like, in the middle of a meeting? Or breakfast?" His voice lowered conspiratorially. "How many times does he even… do that in a day?"

The question hung there, pregnant with possibility. Aidan shifted uncomfortably. His red ears grew even redder as he cleared his throat, avoiding everyone's eyes. "Well… I mean…" Aidan mumbled, running a hand through his hair. "I did… I did hear something this morning." Everyone in the shed instantly stopped what they were doing. Eric leaned forward, his eyes wide with anticipation. Mark swung back around, a wide, predatory grin on his face. Lily arched a brow, a silent dare in her expression.

Aidan swallowed hard, glancing at Alissa, who was now openly staring at him, a mixture of shock and morbid curiosity on her face. "Okay, look. It was, uh… In the main house. Early morning, maybe six, six-thirty. I was getting ready for the morning meeting, David, obviously, had just left his room." He paused, taking a deep breath like a man about to dive into cold water. "And then… then I heard it. From the pantry."

A collective gasp rippled through the small group. "The pantry?" Eric whispered, his eyes gleaming. Aidan nodded. "Yeah. The pantry. I heard… noises." He gestured vaguely, as if the noises themselves were too scandalous to name. "And then I heard Elena's voice. Apparently, she just started the coffee, and he was definitely giving it to her, hard." Lily let out a low whistle. "Bold. I like it."

Josh threw his head back and laughed, a booming sound that echoed in the metal shed. "See, Marvin? I told you! That's David's style. Surprise and… appreciation. You know, I wouldn't be surprised if Tiffany was getting plowed over a bale of hay as we speak." He winked broadly. "She's always had a thing for being taken… 'unwillingly,' if you catch my drift. Says it adds to the thrill."

Marvin looked utterly bewildered, his eyes darting between Josh and the others, trying to decipher if this was all an elaborate prank or the honest, unvarnished truth of life with David. Alissa, wiping a tear of laughter from her eye, leaned into Aidan, shaking her head. "You know, it all makes sense now." She looked around at the group, her expression settling into one of amused resignation. "Jennifer, you hardly ever see her wearing underwear." She paused, a smirk playing on her lips. "And now I understand why."

Just as Alissa finished her thought, a mischievous glint entered her eye. Without saying another word, a sudden burst of energy seized her. She turned on her heel and, much to the surprise of the others, darted out of the work shed, her laughter echoing behind her. Aidan watched her go, a slow smile spreading across his face. "Well, I guess some things just need to be confirmed firsthand," he chuckled, shaking his head.

Lily leaned against a stack of what looked like fence posts, her arms crossed, a knowing smirk on her face. "She's heading for the barn, isn't she?" she mused, more to herself than anyone else. Eric scratched his chin, a thoughtful, almost academic expression on his face. "It's remarkable, really. His ability to maintain such… enthusiastic marital relations across so many partners. One would think the logistics alone would be a nightmare. And the energy! He's what, pushing fifty? David's clearly on a different plane."

Just then, Alissa reappeared in the doorway of the shed, her chest heaving slightly, a wild, almost disbelieving look on her face. She was shaking her head slowly, a hand pressed over her mouth, but a faint, uncontrollable giggle bubbled up from behind it. "Well?" Aidan asked, leaning forward, an expectant grin on his face. "What did you see? Was Josh right? Is Mom… doing the hay thing?"

Alissa took a deep, shuddering breath, her eyes wide as she finally managed to control her laughter enough to speak. "Aidan," she gasped, her voice a mix of awe and utter bewilderment, "it wasn't just Tiffany this time." She paused, taking another breath, as if steeling herself for the next revelation. "Nicole was in the barn too." The shed fell silent for a beat. Then another.

Josh's eyes widened, a slow, triumphant smile spreading across his face. "No way! The 'sex sandwich'?! I fucking told you!" He slammed his hand down on a nearby workbench with a resounding slap. "I literally just said it! I'm a prophet! Call me Josh-tradamus!" Marvin cleared his throat awkwardly. "So… this is just… a thing, then? The barn? And the… the multiple wives at once?" He looked from Alissa to Aidan, then to Lily. "Has this ever happened to you guys? Like, you just… walk in on David with one or more of his wives? And how do you… how do you even react to that?"

Aidan shrugged. "Honestly, dude? Yeah, it's always been normal. Since I was old enough to, well, understand what was going on, it's just been… part of life in our family. Dad's very… affectionate. And he's got a lot of wives who are very… affectionate back." Lily nodded. "It's what we call 'shameless affection,' Marvin. It's actually encouraged. David believes that love isn't something to hide away.

Aidan chuckled. "Look, it's less about the where and more about the why. Dad… he processes things differently. He's brilliant, but expressing emotion, especially affection, isn't always something that comes naturally to him in the typical way. It's like his brain has to reroute the signals through a logic processor first, and by the time it comes out, it's… intense. And often, it comes out in physical ways, in moments of unguarded comfort."

Lily lowered her head. "Exactly. David has difficulty showing affection normally, because of how he thinks. It's not that he doesn't feel it, he feels it profoundly, it's just that the expression of it is a conscious, sometimes difficult, act for him. So, when he does open up, when he lets that affection flow freely, it's a big deal. It's a moment of pure, unadulterated vulnerability and connection." She met Marvin's gaze directly. "And when he does, it's best to just let him. You don't question it, you don't interrupt it, and you certainly don't make him feel ashamed for it."

Josh, who had been pacing excitedly, stopped suddenly, pointing a finger at Marvin. "And here's the kicker, Marv! If you do reject David's affection, you risk losing it forever. Not because he's petty, or punishes you, but because it's such a hard thing for him to give in the first place. It's like… a fragile, rare bird. If it flies to you and you shoo it away, it might just decide it's safer to stay hidden."

Lily nodded vigorously. "Exactly! Now, let me ask you somethin', Marv. You ever heard David ramble on about that time he… re-experienced his whole life? Or about his 'regression'?" Josh leaned in, his eyes wide with theatrical mystery. Marvin blinked. "Regression? Yeah, vaguely. Junior mentioned it once, something about him living his life over. Sounded pretty out there, honestly. Like, a sci-fi movie plot. I kinda figured it was just David being… David, with his metaphors and deep thoughts."

Josh threw his hands up in mock exasperation. "See?! See, that's what I'm talkin' about! It ain't no metaphor, Marv! Not in the way you're thinkin'! David, our David, lived through all this before. He's got all that knowledge, all that experience, every single memory of a whole life, shoved into his brain. And he remembers it all. The good, the bad, the ugly… and the painful." He began pacing again, but slower this time.

"So, imagine this," Josh continued, turning back to Marvin. "You got a guy, brilliant, capable, who's got this massive heart, but he struggles to show it. Why, you ask? Because he learned not to. He learned that showing that kind of emotion, that deep affection, could be used as a weapon." He paused, looking around at the small group. "Well, let me tell you, Marv, that ain't no metaphor. See, in that first go-round, my mama… Lynn. Sweetest lady you ever met now, right? Always worrying, always making sure you've eaten. But back then, in David's first life… he was her husband, and she wasn't so warm to him. Not cold, exactly, but she just… couldn't accept him the way he needed."

Josh's voice softened, losing some of its boisterousness. "David, being David, was always different, even as a kid. He was a puzzle, a whirlwind of intelligence and unique ways of seeing the world. And she… well, she just kept pushing him away, emotionally speakin'. Every time he tried to show her he loved her, every time he tried to get close, she'd put up a wall. Not on purpose, maybe. She probably didn't even realize she was doing it, or the damage it was causing. But she did it. Repeatedly. And that, my friend, that burned him. Deep."

"Woah," Marvin breathed. "Lynn? David was… married to Lynn? And she doesn't even remember? That's… that's messed up, Josh." He glanced towards Eric and Mark, who were staring at Josh with expressions ranging from bewildered amusement to outright disbelief. "Lynn knows," Josh said, his voice low. "They both do. It was weird for a while. I could always feel it, somethin'… off. A tension. Like Mama stole his CD collection, but I never knew why. Then, one day, they had a long talk, it was different. Still respectful, still some distance, but… there was acceptance there. Closure."

Marvin paused, thinking. "Wait a minute. Lily…" He looked sharply at Josh. "David saved Lynn because of Lily, didn't he?" Josh nodded. "Caught on, huh? Yeah. Because I married Lily, he couldn't just let her die." Eric chuckled, shaking his head. "So, let me get this straight. David, our all-knowing, apocalypse-surviving David, is basically going around rewriting history for the better?" "In a way, yeah," Josh replied. "He's got a second chance. And he's using it to fix things. Not everything, mind you. He can't just wave a magic wand and undo the past. But where he can… he does."

Mark, who had been silent until now, spoke up. "What about Margaret and Clarence? Do they know?" Josh sighed. "Nope. They're blissfully ignorant. David figures, what good would it do to tell them? It would just complicate things, cause unnecessary pain. Pee paw is already a grumpy old coot as it is. Can you imagine him if he found out David used to be married to his daughter?"

Josh chuckled, shaking his head. "You think that's crazy? That barely scratches the surface. The real shocker? Tanya." He paused, letting the name hang in the air. Mark, who had been quietly sipping his coffee, perked up. "Tanya? As in, David's wife, Tanya?" He looked at Alissa, a slight flicker of confusion on his face. "Yep," Josh confirmed, nodding slowly. "Tanya. That's a story, if I've ever heard one. You guys are sitting down, right?"

The group exchanged curious glances. Eric leaned forward, his eyebrows raised expectantly. "Lay it on us, Josh. What's so special about Tanya?" Josh took a deep breath, his expression turning serious. "Alright. This is gonna sound… unbelievable. But remember, we're talking about David." He cleared his throat. "In his previous life… David killed Tanya." "What?!" Marvin exploded, his eyes wide with disbelief. "He… what? You're saying David… murdered Tanya?"

Josh held up his hands defensively. "Woah, woah, hold on a minute. It wasn't… malicious. It was… mercy." He struggled for the right words. "She was in terrible pain, riddled with disease at 43, suffering horribly. There weren't any doctors, no medicine, nothing. David, being David, couldn't stand to see her suffer. He said he would end her pain, and then…ended it." He winced, the words hanging heavy in the air. "He said he cut her head off."

Eric stared at Josh, mouth agape. Mark rubbed his temples, looking utterly bewildered. Finally, Alissa spoke, her voice a hesitant whisper. "But… this time he found her, perfectly healthy." Josh nodded. "Exactly! This time, knowing what was coming, he went looking for her. Found her working at some studio in Seattle. Saved her. Brought her back here." He spread his hands, gesturing around the ranch. "Now they're married. And she couldn't be happier."

Marvin, still reeling from the revelation, sputtered, "But...does she know? Does Tanya know that David...that he..." He gestured with his finger. Josh sighed. "Yeah, Marvin. She knows." The silence stretched, thick with disbelief and morbid curiosity. Mark finally broke it, "So, you're telling me...Tanya is married to the guy who chopped her head off in a past life? And she's okay with that?"

Josh nodded slowly. "More than okay. She understands. In fact, I'd say she's one of David's most devoted wives." He paused a moment. "Look, I wish I was making it up. It sounds insane, I know. But I swear, it's true. David told me himself. And Tanya was right there when he was telling me the story, laying her head in his lap the whole time."

Eric, sighed. "Alright, alright, enough with the soap opera reenactments. Mulching calls. Besides," he added, "I don't think my past life ended with David's hand." Lily tugged at Josh's sleeve. "Honey, we really need to get back to the compost. You know how David gets when the system's running behind." She shot a pointed glance at the overflowing bin.

Josh, relieved at the distraction, clapped Marvin on the shoulder. "Look, pal, I get it. Lots of fascinating stories. But the important part is, we're all here." Marvin, however, wasn't letting it go. The gears in his young mind were visibly grinding. "But...are there more? Are there other... incidents? Did he used to run a pirate ship? Was he a Roman Emperor? Tell me there's a pirate ship story!"

Mark, who had been quietly sipping his coffee, suddenly piped up "What about you, Aidan? Have you ever asked your mother about David? I mean, she was wife number one, right? She must have some juicy stories." Aidan raised an eyebrow, "Actually, mom is more or less the historian. She probably knows more than anyone."

Mark, ever the instigator, turned his attention to Aidan. "So, what's the deal? Any juicy details from your mom, the OG wife?" Aidan took a sip of his coffee, leaning against a stack of fence posts. "Actually, mom is the family historian. She probably knows more than anyone." Alissa, handing out the last of the cookies, chimed in, "That's true. David kept detailed journals of everything he remembered from his... previous iteration. Tiffany was the first one to decrypt them."

A collective gasp rippled through the group. "He wrote it all down?" Eric asked, intrigued despite himself. "In code," Alissa clarified. "A code that only his wives and children know." As she and Aidan gathered the empty mugs to leave, she turned back. "It's not that deep, it's just a journal."

Chapter 7:

Consent and Growing Pains

"Five more minutes," Alissa mumbled, her face buried in his chest. "Date night is coming up, and I'm not ready." Aidan chuckled, gently prying her arms away. "Date night is two weeks away, and you were going to spend today with Tiffany. Besides, Tyler needs to go to school soon. He slipped out of bed and began getting dressed. He kissed Alissa on the forehead and slipped out the door. Her last words were a reminder to get ready for date night and that she would see him later when Tiffany was done with her.

Meanwhile, a few apartments over, Kyle was experiencing a far different wake-up call. He blinked, trying to focus on the figure standing at the foot of his bed. It was Taylor, and she was holding his discarded jeans. "Good morning, sleepyhead," she purred, a mischievous look in her eyes. Kyle's heart hammered against his ribs. He glanced around wildly, half-expecting to see David lurking in the shadows, ready to unleash the wrath of a betrayed husband. "Taylor, what are you doing here? What if David finds out?"

Taylor merely shrugged, her expression unapologetic. "He won't. Besides," she added with a sly smile, "I think you'll enjoy what I have planned." Before Kyle could protest, she leaned over and whispered something in his ear that made his eyes widen. He gulped, his initial panic slowly giving way to a potent cocktail of apprehension and… well, curiosity.

The next thing he knew, Taylor was expertly tying his wrists to the bedposts with one of his belts. As she stepped back to admire her handiwork, Kyle's panic returned with a vengeance. "Taylor, seriously! What are you doing?" he sputtered, tugging at the restraints. "This isn't funny." Taylor tilted her head. "Oh, I think it's hilarious. And…educational. Tell me, Kyle, when you were teaching Junior, did you ever…notice me?"

Kyle's face flushed. "What? That was twelve years ago, Taylor! I… I don't even remember." "Really?" Taylor's voice was soft, almost disbelieving. She took a step closer. "Because I remember you. I remember the way you looked at me when you thought I wasn't watching. The little…hesitations you had when you handed me a drink. The jealousy in your eyes when David had his way with me."

Kyle swallowed hard. He could feel the sweat beading on his forehead. "Taylor, please. This isn't right. David trusts you." He barely recognized his own voice. Taylor's smile faltered, replaced by a flicker of vulnerability. "Does he, Kyle? Does he really? Or am I just another number in his collection? Another woman he picked because…well, because he could?" She reached out and brushed a stray strand of hair from his forehead, her touch sending another jolt of electricity through him. "I deserve to be desired, Kyle. Not just…owned."

He wanted to argue, to tell her she was wrong, that David genuinely cared for each of his wives. But the words caught in his throat, choked by the undeniable truth of her statement. He'd seen the way David operated. He knew the power he wielded, the quiet authority that influenced every aspect of life on the ranch. "Taylor, stop," he begged, his voice barely a whisper. "You don't want to do this. It'll ruin everything."

Taylor ignored Kyle's plea. Her eyes, usually bright and cheerful, were shadowed with a complex mix of hurt and determination. She rummaged in her purse, pulling out a small, black, ball gag. Kyle recognized it instantly. It was one of Kayla's...novelties. His eyes widened in terror. "Taylor..." he mumbled, trying to shake his head. But she was already on him, gently but firmly placing the ball gag in his mouth and securing it behind his head. The leather straps felt cold against his skin. He thrashed against the restraints, a muffled scream building in his throat. Panic clawed at him, a suffocating wave. He couldn't believe this was happening. Not with Taylor.

Taylor watched him struggle, a strange sadness in her eyes. "I'm sorry, Kyle," she whispered, her voice barely audible above his muffled protests. "I don't want to hurt you. But you need to listen. You need to see me." She reached for the hem of her simple cotton dress, her fingers trembling slightly. With a slow, deliberate motion, she pulled it over her head, letting it fall to the floor.

Taylor watched Kyle's frantic struggle, a tear tracing a path down her cheek. She reached out, gently stroking his cheek. "Shhh, Kyle, shhh. It's okay. I'm not going to hurt you. I would never betray David. You know that." Her voice was soft, a calming balm against the storm of his panic.

She leaned closer, her voice barely a whisper in the small apartment. "This…this isn't real, Kyle. Not exactly.

You've been…alone, haven't you? You haven't been with a woman, since Arizona? Too busy playing protector for everyone, too busy with those damn guns. Too busy waiting for that girl to grow up?" She moved a hand down to his chest. "Your body remembers, though. I see it in your eyes when I am around you. I feel it in how you act. Your body remembers how it likes to be treated."

Taylor stepped back slightly, gesturing toward him with a sad smile. "This is your mind playing tricks on you. A dream. A fantasy, maybe. A way to cope with…well, with everything. So, relax. Let your imagination treat you for once." Taylor stood back, her own nakedness a stark contrast to the morning's serenity. The image of her body, usually bringing him comfort and joy in passing, now felt like a brand on his skin. He couldn't reconcile the soft, caring Taylor he knew with the woman who had just... gagged him.

His eyes darted to the sheet covering him, or rather, not covering him. He was completely exposed. He tugged at the restraints, a desperate, muffled plea escaping the confines of the ball gag. His heart hammered against his ribs, a frantic drumbeat against the silence of the room. Then, he saw it.

His eyes snapped back to Taylor, his gaze snagging on her hips, her breasts, her neck. His mind, a chaotic mess moments before, began to slowly focus. The dream like nature of it, like she said, was very clear. His body, traitor that it was, responded immediately. Despite the fear, the confusion, and the sheer wrongness of the situation, an undeniable stirring began.

Taylor watched him, a mixture of sadness and something akin to amusement flickering in her eyes. She knelt beside the bed, reaching out to gently stroke his cheek. "There you are," she murmured, her voice soft as silk. "I knew you were still in there, hiding behind all that duty and responsibility. It is okay to treat yourself for once."

She leaned closer, her breath warm against his ear. "Don't fight it, Kyle. This is a gift. A chance to let go, to feel something other than the weight of the world on your shoulders. You have my permission." She moved her hand a fraction lower, tracing a line down his chest, stopping just above his belly button. His breath hitched. "Remember," she whispered, her voice a gentle invitation, "this is your fantasy. What do you want to happen next?"

Kyle lifted his hands from his side, as if they were never bound, then reached for his mouth. There was no ball gag. He blinked, the remnants of a deeply disturbing, yet also… strangely compelling dream clinging to his consciousness. He was still naked, the air in the room thick with the scent of vanilla and something subtly… charged.

His eyes focused on Taylor again, who was now forcing her throat over his cock. Kyle's breath hitched. This was… terrifyingly unreal. He tried to speak, to stammer out a protest, a question, anything, but the attempt died in his throat. She was… dedicated. Determined. As Kyle's mind wandered, trying to piece together what was happening, David walked in, leaving his door wide open.

"Good morning!" David said, cheerfully. "I see you get to have your day started right." David, looking impossibly fresh-faced and radiating an aura of amusement, strolled further into the room, casually picking up a magazine from the bedside table. Kyle's eyes widened in full blown panic. He tried to speak, but all that came out was a high-pitched squeaking sound.

Taylor paused, glancing up. "Morning, Daddy," she said, with a completely straight face. "Just ensuring Kyle gets some... personalized attention. He's been working so hard lately." She said, then smoothly resumed her task. Kyle's entire being rebelled. The term "Daddy" coming from Taylor's lips felt like a perversion, a violation of some unwritten, fundamental law of the universe. He squeezed his eyes shut, trying to block out the sight, the sound, the feeling of what was happening.

But he couldn't. He was trapped, a prisoner in his own body, forced to endure this surreal dream. He opened his eyes again, his gaze darting frantically around the room, searching for an escape, a sign of reality. David stood unbothered, flipping through the pages of the magazine. And then... he came.

The release was sudden, overwhelming, a tidal wave of sensation that washed over him, momentarily silencing the chaos in his mind. Shame, confusion, and a disconcerting surge of pleasure warred within him. He could feel her... sucking, never slowing down. He looked for David, but his door was shut, the magazine still on his nightstand. As his eyes focused on the woman on top of him, he recognized her hair instantly. It wasn't Taylor, it never was. It was Grace.

Grace, with a mischievous glint in her eyes, turned and kissed him hard on the mouth, a firm, lingering kiss that sent his brain spiraling further into the abyss. "Good morning, Darling," she said, her voice a little too knowing, a little too… adult. Then, with a giggle, she hopped off the bed and darted out the door. It clicked shut behind her, leaving him alone in the aftermath of the most surreal, disturbing, and strangely… memorable… experience of his life.

The morning sun, a pale intruder through the LCD screen window mimicking a sunrise, did little to dispel the fog in Kyle's brain. He sat bolt upright in bed, sheets tangled around his waist, the remnants of the… thing that just happened still clinging to him like a bad cologne. Grace's shoes. Bright pink Crocs, adorned with little charms shaped like firearms, sat innocently on the floor next to his bed. They were irrefutable evidence. This wasn't some fever dream born of canned fruit and apocalyptic anxieties.

He ran a hand through his hair, which, he realized, was plastered to his forehead with a sheen of… something. He didn't want to think about it. He really, really didn't want to think about it. A knock echoed on his door. Kyle froze, heart hammering against his ribs. He knew instinctively who it was. "Darling? You awake?" Grace's voice, high and sweet, dripped with a faux-innocence that sent shivers down his spine.

Kyle swallowed hard, trying to regain some semblance of composure. "Uh… yeah, Grace. Just… uh… give me a minute!" He scrambled out of bed, pulling on a pair of cargo shorts. He glanced in the mirror, horrified. His face was flushed, his eyes wide and wild. He looked like he'd just wrestled a badger. A very happy badger.

Another knock, more insistent this time. "But Darling, breakfast will get cold! I made your favorite – pancakes with whipped cream!" Pancakes. His traitorous stomach rumbled. He did like pancakes. Damn her culinary manipulations! Grace didn't wait. She unlocked the door from the outside and immediately stepped in. She nervously looked at her shoes and quickly stepped into them, holding out a plate of pancakes. "Here you go, Darling. I even added extra whipped cream, just how you like it." She beamed, her eyes sparkling with an unsettling mixture of affection and… victory?

Kyle nervously took the plate. He was a grown man. He should be able to handle a 15-year-old's infatuation. Especially one involving breakfast. "Thanks, Grace," he mumbled, taking a tentative bite. The pancakes were, admittedly, delicious. Light, fluffy, and swimming in whipped cream. He took another bite. And another. He was starving.

"So," Grace said, leaning against the doorframe, a sly smile playing on her lips. "Did you sleep well, Darling?" Kyle choked on a mouthful of pancake. "Uh… yeah. Great. Slept like a… log." He mentally face-palmed. A log? Really? Kyle, still chewing with his mouth open, managed to speak, "Grace, look… these are amazing pancakes, seriously. Best I've had since… ever." He gestured vaguely with his fork, trying to distract from the redness creeping up his neck. "But… you can't… you can't just keep sneaking in here when I'm, uh, sleeping."

Grace tilted her head, her brow furrowing slightly, but the sly smile remained. "But Darling, I only do it to take care of you! You work so hard all the time. You need your rest, and a good breakfast to start the day. Besides," she added with a conspiratorial whisper, "who else is going to make sure you're properly taken care of?"

Kyle ran a hand through his already messy hair. This was like a bizarre, whipped-cream-fueled hostage situation. "Grace, I appreciate the thought, really. But I'm a grown man. I can make my own breakfast. And... and lock my own doors." He emphasized the last part, giving the door a pointed look. "But Darling," Grace protested, stepping closer. "It's fun! And I want to be a good wife! Like making the perfect pancakes, and... and keeping you comfortable." She batted her eyelashes, an effect that would have been charming if Kyle wasn't acutely aware of her intentions.

"Grace, being a good wife is about more than pancakes and... and breaking and entering," Kyle said, trying to keep his voice steady. "It's about... about mutual respect, and communication, and... and definitely not sneaking into someone's apartment at 6 AM!" "I do respect you, Kyle," she said softly, her voice losing its playful edge. "No one will ever respect you as much as I do, and I thought... well, I hoped you'd enjoy the... extra bit of attention. Besides, who wouldn't appreciate a good blowjob first thing in the morning." She saw the blood drain from Kyle's face and immediately regretted her bluntness.

"Okay, okay," Grace said quickly, holding up her hands. "I get it. Too much. I'm sorry. Just... I want to show you how much I care." She bit her lip, her usual confidence faltering. "I understand how frustrated you must be, and I wanted to help, without crossing 'that' line." Kyle looked at her, a complex mix of exasperation and… something akin to tenderness washing over him. He knew she was just trying to express her feelings, however misguided her methods.

"Grace," he sighed, "I appreciate the sentiment. But we need to talk. About… about boundaries, and expectations, and… and the fact that you're fifteen." Grace crossed her arms, her chin lifting slightly. "I know how old I am, Kyle. And I know what I want. And I know what you want, too." "Grace…" "Look," she interrupted, "I know it's… unconventional. And everyone's going to have something to say, no matter how long I wait. So what's the point in waiting?"

Kyle's silence was damning. "Jessica is also seventeen years younger than David and she's his favorite." Grace added, trying to sway him. Kyle groaned inwardly. Bringing the dynamics of David's unconventional family into this was just making things worse. "That's… that's different, Grace. David's… David's David. I'm just… Kyle."

Grace stepped closer, her voice dropping to a whisper. "But you're my Kyle." She reached up and gently brushed a stray strand of hair from his forehead. "And I know you want this just as much as I do." Kyle closed his eyes for a moment, fighting the urge to just give in. He did want her. He was attracted to her. She was intelligent, perceptive, and had the mind of a grown woman. But he didn't want to betray David's trust.

"Grace," he said softly, opening his eyes, "I do care about you. A lot. But... I can't. I just can't. It's not right." Grace's eyes narrowed. "Right? What's right got to do with anything anymore? The world ended, Kyle! Everyone's making a choice of their own free will, and this is mine!" Her voice rose in pitch. "You're always thinking about what other people might think! Always so concerned about appearances! About what the 'readers' are going to say!"

Kyle flinched, the accusation hitting a nerve. He was concerned about the optics. He was acutely aware that their relationship, even just as friends, was already raising eyebrows. Grace saw his reaction and pressed her advantage. "Honestly Kyle, if the readers were going to be offended by this," she said with a defiant glint in her eyes, "they wouldn't have made it past the first book."

Kyle stared at her, speechless. She had a point. This wasn't some prim and proper Regency romance. This was an erotic science fiction rom-com, a genre that, by its very nature, often played with societal boundaries. Since when does the author care about social norms? "Okay," he said. "Okay, you're right. I... I might be overthinking this. But Grace, you have to understand... people talk. And David..." He trailed off, picturing David's knowing, slightly amused gaze.

Grace softened, her anger dissipating. "I know, Kyle. I do. It's just... I'm tired of being treated like a kid." She stepped closer and placed a hand on his arm. "Can we... can we compromise?" Kyle blinked. A compromise? He hadn't even considered that. He'd been so focused on drawing a hard line in the sand, trying to protect Grace, himself, and the already fragile social equilibrium of the ranch, that he hadn't thought about finding a middle ground. "How?" he asked, his voice laced with wary curiosity. "How do we compromise on something like this, Grace?"

"Well," she began, her eyes sparkling with a newfound determination. "I promise I won't sneak into your apartment when you're sleeping anymore. No more sneaky blowjobs," she added, almost as an afterthought, as if it were a minor detail. "And I won't urge you to have sex with me anymore. I promise." Kyle stared at her, a wave of relief washing over him. Those were promises he could definitely live with. He nodded slowly, cautiously. "Okay. That's… that's a good start, Grace."

"But," she continued, her tone shifting, becoming more serious, more… womanly. "In exchange, I want to be able to kiss you. And hold you. And just… be with you. In private, like a real woman. You don't have to reciprocate yet, Kyle. Just… allow me to be who I am." Kyle's breath hitched. "Grace," he began, his voice a little shaky. "That's… still asking a lot."

"But it's not like I'm playing games with you, Kyle," she said, her gaze steady, earnest. "David trusts me implicitly, you know he does. He knows I'm not some flighty child. I'm going to be your wife, Kyle. Just like Jessica dreamed of David when she was thirteen. Her future with him was certain, so why can't we accept our own future in the same way? I Know I'm meant to be with you."

He looked at Grace, really looked at her. She was young, yes, but there was an undeniable maturity in her eyes. She looked at him with such… certainty. It was both terrifying and, he had to admit, a little bit flattering. "You really think it's that certain?" he asked. Grace's smile was radiant, a beacon in the dim room. "I know it, Kyle. I knew I was going to marry you the day you came back, three years ago."

She paused, her eyes scanning his face. "And since I can't magically appear in your space without you knowing, I'm going to need your explicit permission to enter your apartment whenever I want, so I don't have to sneak in anymore." Kyle blinked. Explicit permission. It was the most formal request he'd ever received for something so intensely personal. Stop her? He might as well try to stop the sun from rising. She'd find a way, he was sure of it.

He sighed, a sound of weary resignation that was quickly followed by a surge of something akin to acceptance. "Okay, Grace," he said, his voice low. "You have my explicit permission." The effect was instantaneous. Grace launched herself into his arms, a whirlwind of excitement, her small body surprisingly strong. Her lips found his, a kiss that was at once intimate and incredibly knowing, a promise of things to come that sent a surprising jolt through him. Her arms wrapped around his neck, pulling him closer, and for a moment, in the shared intimacy of the kiss, everything else seemed to vanish.

When she finally pulled back, her cheeks were flushed, her eyes shining with triumph and a possessive satisfaction.

She looked up at him, a slow, languid smile spreading across her face. "Just so you know, your cum is delicious, Kyle," she murmured, before pushing away from him and practically bouncing out of his apartment, leaving him standing there, stunned, the lingering taste of her kiss on his lips and a whole lot of questions swirling in his mind.

In Apartment 2, the aroma of slightly burnt toast mingled with the comforting scent of coffee. Eric, still in his worn pajamas, watched his daughter, Bonnie, with a bemused expression. The twelve-year-old was meticulously applying a sheer lip gloss, her brow furrowed in concentration. A delicate, almost imperceptible dusting of something shimmery adorned her eyelids. "Morning, sunshine," Eric said, his voice raspy with sleep. He poured himself a mug of coffee, the dark liquid a welcome jolt. "Getting all dolled up for breakfast?"

Bonnie jumped slightly, startled. She quickly closed the lip gloss with a snap. "Morning, Daddy," she chirped, her voice a little higher than usual. Her hand instinctively went to her chest, where a slight, but noticeable, curve was beginning to form beneath her oversized t-shirt. A genuine, unrestrained smile bloomed on her face. "I get to wear a bra today!" she announced, bouncing in her seat.

Eric's eyebrows rose. "A bra? That's... exciting, honey. Are you sure about that?" Bonnie nodded enthusiastically, her eyes, still rimmed with the faint sparkle of makeup, sparkling with a different kind of light. "Yep! Nicole and Summer were showing me how to put them on yesterday. And they told me about... about other things too.

Like, how to deal with… stuff." She gestured vaguely, a blush creeping up her neck.

Eric chuckled softly, a warm, deep sound. He appreciated this. He truly did. Ever since the EMP had plunged the world into this new, quieter existence, the concept of "raising a daughter" had felt like navigating uncharted territory. He'd been so worried about how he'd manage, but then Nicole and Summer, and even Summer's daughter Lily, had so readily stepped in. They'd taken Bonnie under their wing, sharing their wisdom about becoming a woman. He'd always known his ex-wife would have been thrilled to see Bonnie surrounded by such capable women.

He glanced at the small, delicate diamond ring on Bonnie's left hand. It was still a bit surreal, the whole arrangement with Seth. He hadn't been keen on the idea of his twelve-year-old daughter being "betrothed," even if it was in this strange, post-apocalyptic world. But Seth had a maturity beyond his years. And the way he looked at Bonnie, with such genuine affection and respect, had slowly won Eric over.

"Well, that's great, sweetie," Eric said, taking a sip of his coffee. "Just… make sure it's comfortable, okay? We don't want you fidgeting all day." He didn't miss the way Bonnie's hand still unconsciously smoothed down the front of her shirt. He knew she was eager to embrace this new chapter, this transition into young womanhood. And he was committed to preparing her, ensuring she was a strong, capable woman, worthy of the future he envisioned for her, a future where she could stand on her own two feet, even if that future involved a husband like Seth.

Bonnie beamed, her youthful enthusiasm infectious as she snagged a piece of toast that had finally cooled enough to eat. "It is! And Seth is going to be teaching about the women of World War II today at school. Isn't that cool? He says they were really strong." Eric nodded, a wry smile playing on his lips. Seth's lessons were always… interesting. He had a remarkable knack for unearthing historical figures who embodied resilience and strength, qualities he clearly aimed to instill in his intended bride. "That sounds fascinating, honey. I'm sure he'll have some great stories."

Then, with a determined air, Bonnie hopped off the stool and made her way to the small table near the door, where her gear was meticulously laid out. She grabbed her pistol belt, the familiar weight a testament to their transformed reality, and fastened it around her waist. After sliding the keepers down around her belt, securing it in place, she reached for her pistol. With a fluid, practiced motion, she picked up her Sig P365, expertly loaded a magazine, and then holstered it with a soft click. After grabbing and holstering two spare magazines, she slung her backpack over one shoulder. "Bye, Dad!" she called, her voice already heading for the door, her steps eager and purposeful.

Eric watched her go, a flicker of something akin to disbelief crossing his features as he saw Mike emerging from the hallway, his own Glock 19 holstered to his hip. Lori and Beth were close behind, their small forms already radiating a similar readiness for the day's tasks. The sight of his daughter and Mike, armed and heading to school, still managed to elicit a hollow, disbelieving laugh from him. How utterly preposterous their lives had become.

As he turned to head back inside, a familiar figure appeared at the foot of the stairs. Lynn, her face etched with a familiar concern that never quite faded, was walking towards him. "Morning, Eric," she said, her voice soft but clear. Eric offered a slight nod. "Morning, Lynn. Everything alright?"

Lynn approached, her eyes scanning his face as if searching for an answer to a question she hadn't yet voiced. She paused, a tentative expression on her face. "Eric," she began, her voice dropping slightly, "do you think… would it be alright if I came in for a few minutes? I wanted to talk to you about something." Eric gestured vaguely towards the entryway. "Sure, Lynn. Come on in. What's on your mind?" He asked, pushing open the door. "Thanks," Lynn murmured, stepping into his apartment. Eric closed the door behind her, the click echoing softly. He gestured towards the sofa. "Have a seat. Coffee's still warm, if you want some." He moved towards the small kitchenette, already reaching for a mug.

Lynn hesitated for a moment, her gaze sweeping over the apartment, lingering briefly on a framed photo on a side table, him and Bonnie, younger, oblivious to the world that would soon unravel. Then, she sat, perching on the edge of the sofa as if unsure whether she truly belonged there. "No, thank you, Eric," she said, her voice still laced with that gentle uncertainty. She clasped her hands in her lap, her fingers twisting together. "I... I was just thinking about Bonnie."

Eric turned from the counter, mug in hand, and leaned against it. He watched her, a familiar mix of concern and quiet exasperation swirling within him. "She's heading to school, Lynn. Got her gear all packed and ready, just like always." He took a sip of his coffee. Lynn nodded, her eyes fixed on her hands. "I know. And it's... it's amazing, isn't it? How adaptable they are. How quickly they just... accept. Josh too.

Lynn let out a soft sigh. "It's just... sometimes I watch them. Bonnie, Josh, Mike, even Lori and Beth," she chuckled softly at the thought. "And I see how prepared they are, how well they adapted. And then I think about... about my life before." She looked directly at him, her expression tinged with a wistfulness he knew all too well. "I remember the safety, the ease. The assumption that everything would just... work. And then I think about how I wasn't prepared for it when it didn't. How I struggled to adapt, to let go of expectations."

Eric pushed off the counter, setting his mug down. He walked over and sat beside her on the sofa, a comfortable distance between them. He kept his tone gentle, devoid of judgment. "We all made mistakes, Lynn. We all had our own ways of dealing with it. You were used to a certain... stability. It's a hard habit to break when the ground beneath you falls out."

Lynn finally looked at him, a flicker of hope in her eyes. "But I want to break it, Eric. I want to learn. I see how David manages everything, how he anticipates, how he cares for everyone. And I see you, too. You've always been so steady, so capable. You helped me get my parents back, you've always been there for Bonnie. You're a good man, Eric."

Her hands unclasped, and she tentatively reached out, placing one on his forearm. Her touch was light, almost hesitant. "And I was thinking… about date night. Next Saturday." She swallowed, her cheeks flushing slightly. "And I was wondering… if you might consider… if you would want to be my date, Eric?"

The question hung in the quiet air, unexpected and yet, in a strange way, a natural progression of their shared history. Eric looked at her, at the sincerity in her eyes, the genuine desire to move forward, to embrace the present. He saw not the woman who had clung to the past, but the one who was actively reaching for a brighter future, even if it was a future built on entirely different foundations. Eric nodded, "Of course I will."

Chapter 8:

Date Night: Early Noon

Tonight, the air thrummed with a different kind of energy on the ranch, date night. And as usual, the smallest members of their sprawling family were being corralled. Aidan, looking surprisingly put-together in a clean shirt, entered the main house. In his arms, a napping four-month-old Tyler, a precious bundle of quiet. He found Kathy and Taylor already in their element. "Hey, ladies," Aidan chirped, carefully depositing Tyler into a bassinet. "Hoping for a few hours of non-diaper related activities tonight."

Kathy was meticulously organizing a mountain of brightly colored building blocks. Her expression was one of serene efficiency. "Don't worry, Aidan. These little ones are mostly just practicing their lung capacity at the moment. We've got them covered." Taylor, her arms laden with a suspiciously large collection of stuffed animals, offered a warm, crinkled smile. "He's a good little sleeper, isn't he, Kathy?" Taylor murmured. "Almost a shame to wake him from his tiny, adorable nightmares."

Sara, her usual determined stride softened by the precious cargo she carried, deposited a yawning Jake into a playpen. The seven-month-old, already a connoisseur of whatever was within reach, immediately dove headfirst into the colorful pit balls, his chubby hands flailing with glee.

Lucas, meanwhile, was already securely ensconced in his own little corner, utterly absorbed in a world of squeaky toys.

In another part of the sprawling garage complex, Tiffany and Elena were engaged in their own form of child-wrangling. The space had been transformed into a vibrant haven for the older children, filled with craft supplies and board games. Beth, eight and fiercely independent, was meticulously gluing sequins onto a paper crown, her brow furrowed in concentration. Her younger sister, Lori, a whirlwind of giggles and energy, was trying to coax a reluctant stuffed elephant into a game of Go Fish.

Jessica arrived with Poppy, her eight-month-old daughter. Poppy, a creature of discerning tastes, was clearly unimpressed by the offerings of baby toys. Instead, she surveyed the scene with a regal air, her dark blue eyes sweeping over the colorful chaos before settling on a quiet corner. Jessica, with a knowing smirk, tossed Poppy into another pit ball-filled playpen, where she promptly settled down with a small stack of books, her tiny fingers tracing the illustrations with an almost scholarly intensity.

Aidan maneuvered the beast out of the garage. Beside him, Alissa hummed a contented tune, a rare moment of escape from her usual duties. "Are you sure about this, Aidan?" Alissa asked, her eyes scanning the driveway in front of them. "Bonnie's going to practically vibrate out of her seat with excitement, and Seth will probably be too busy trying to play it cool to actually enjoy himself." Aidan reached over and squeezed her hand. "Let them have their teenage romance.

Plus, we're getting a break, and they get to play Romeo and Juliet at a tourist trap." He grinned.

Bonnie, perched in the backseat, was trying for an air of sophistication that was undermined by the barely suppressed bounce in her knees. Beside her, Seth sat stiffly, his hands clasped in his lap, his gaze fixed somewhere beyond the windshield. He caught Bonnie's eye and offered a small, almost imperceptible nod, which she returned with a breathless sigh.

"This car is so amazing, Aidan," Bonnie finally managed, her voice a little higher than usual. "It's like… a spaceship, but for driving on the ground!" Aidan chuckled. "Glad you approve, Bonnie. Just try not to spill anything on the upholstery. It's harder to clean than you'd think." Alissa turned in her seat, a fond smile on her face. "Just enjoy yourselves, you two. Don't worry about impressing anyone. Just be yourselves."

The miles melted away under the Beast's powerful engine, the Texas landscape blurring into streaks of green and gold. The air inside the car was thick with the unspoken sweetness of burgeoning romance and the quiet contentment of respite. As the conversation in the front ebbed and flowed, a silent drama was unfolding in the back. Seth, his usual composure wavering under the magnetic pull of Bonnie's effervescence, felt a sudden, undeniable urge. He glanced at her, her profile illuminated by the passing sun, her hair catching the light. With a deliberate, almost hesitant movement, he reached over. His hand, large and surprisingly gentle for someone so young, hovered for a fraction of a

134

second before descending. He gently took Bonnie's hand, his fingers closing around hers, his thumb resting on the back of her palm.

Bonnie, startled by the unexpected intimacy, looked down at her hand. Her breath hitched. Seth's thumb began to move, tracing slow, delicate circles on her skin. Each stroke was a feather-light caress, a silent language spoken between them. A blush crept up Bonnie's neck, warming her cheeks. She didn't pull her hand away. Instead, she tilted her head slightly, her gaze catching Seth's. In his eyes, she saw a reflection of her own burgeoning feelings, a quiet acknowledgment of the invisible thread that was weaving itself between them, stronger and more vibrant than any spoken word.

The silence stretched, charged with unspoken emotion. Bonnie's heart hammered against her ribs. She took a deep breath, then, leaning closer, her voice a whisper, she asked, "Seth?" He turned his head, his brow furrowed slightly, his thumb still stroking her palm. "Yeah, Bonnie?" Bonnie's gaze flickered down to his lips for a fleeting moment, then back to his eyes. Her voice, though soft, held a new note of curiosity, a tentative boldness. "What… what does it feel like?"

Seth's eyes widened slightly, a flicker of surprise, then understanding, passing through them. He looked at their joined hands, then back at her flushed face. A slow, hesitant smile spread across his lips. He wasn't entirely sure what she was asking about, but he thought he had a pretty good idea. He tightened his grip on her hand. "Like… this, maybe?" he murmured, his thumb pausing its movement, instead just gently pressing against her skin. He kept his gaze locked on hers, searching for any sign of discomfort or disapproval.

Bonnie's blush deepened, but she didn't shy away. "No," she whispered, her voice a little breathy. "I mean… kissing. What does it feel like?" Seth tilted his head slightly, a thoughtful expression on his face. "Well," he began, his voice soft and measured, "physically, it can feel different for everyone. Some people are shy when they kiss, some people are brave. Some kisses are neat, while others can be messy. But that's not really why people do it, you know?"

Alissa, observing the exchange with a knowing smile, nudged Aidan. "I think they're beyond my realm of expertise here." Seth, sensing Bonnie's continued, albeit subtle, nervousness, decided on a different approach. He looked at Alissa. "Alissa," he said, "could you maybe hold Bonnie's hand for a moment? Just like this." He guided Bonnie's hand, so it was palm up. Alissa readily complied, her own hand encompassing Bonnie's. "Like this?" she asked, her touch warm and firm.

Bonnie's eyes widened slightly as she murmured, "It feels like… like someone is holding my hand, like they are keeping an eye on me without looking." A small, contented sigh escaped her lips. Seth then gently took Bonnie's hand and held it again, mirroring Alissa's grip. He held her hand the same way, with that same gentle pressure. Bonnie's eyes fluttered closed for a second, a small gasp escaping her. When she opened them, her gaze met Seth's, a newfound wonder in their depths. "It feels like… like you're holding me like a balloon," she breathed, the analogy so perfect and so revealing of her inner feelings that Aidan nearly choked on his own amusement.

Seth's lips curved into a soft smile. He met Bonnie's gaze, a question in his eyes. Bonnie, emboldened by the unique sensation, met his look directly. "Why," she asked, her voice a little stronger now, "why does it feel so different when you hold my hand like that?" Seth's thumb began to trace small circles on the back of her hand, a deliberate, slow movement that sent a shiver through Bonnie. He then gripped her hand firmly, their fingers interlocking, his thumb continuing its gentle massage on the back of her hand.

Bonnie gasped again, a little louder this time. Her cheeks flamed, and she couldn't quite suppress the delighted squeak that escaped her. "Oh! It's… it's making my heart race!" Her eyes were wide with a delightful sort of panic as she watched Seth's thumb continue its ministration. Seth's gaze softened as he continued to hold her hand, his fingers gently tracing the lines of hers. The subtle pressure, the warmth, the intimate connection – it all sent a dizzying, floaty feeling through Bonnie, like she was rising, weightless, on a cloud of pure happiness.

"It's a different kind of feeling, isn't it?" Seth murmured. "When you know the person holding your hand… when you want them to hold it." Bonnie's breath hitched. The words resonated deep within her, a quiet understanding dawning in her young heart. She understood now, in this silent, shared moment, the why behind the gestures she'd observed, the subtle signals of affection and connection. The gentle pressure, the anchoring warmth, it was a silent language, a promise without words.

Grace stood before the small vanity, her reflection staring back with a mixture of anticipation and anxiety. Grace was determined to make date night unforgettable for Kyle. "A little more blush, honey," Jennifer instructed, holding a soft brush loaded with rosy pigment. "Just a touch." Grace, though eager, resisted. "I don't want to look like a clown, Jennifer. Kyle says I'm pretty without it."

Jennifer chuckled. "He says that now. We want him to say it even louder tonight. Besides, a little extra never hurt." Nicole gently intervened. "Jennifer's right, Grace, but let's not overdo it. Subtle is key. You don't want to look like you're trying too hard." Grace sighed, relenting. "I just want him to see me… differently."

Nicole knelt beside her, placing a comforting hand on Grace's knee. "Kyle already adores you, sweetheart. You don't need to change anything for him. Just be yourself, but the best version of yourself." The 'best version' involved a dress Grace had painstakingly chosen, a flowy, floral number that belonged to Taylor, altered to fit Grace's petite frame. It was a tad mature for her age, but that was the point. She'd even convinced Seo-Yeon to give her a mini-makeover tutorial that morning.

"Okay, final touches," Jennifer announced, brandishing a tube of lip gloss. "Just a dab. We're going for 'kissable,' not 'sticky.'" Grace giggled, leaning in as Jennifer applied the gloss. "Do you think he'll…" she trailed off, her cheeks flushing a delicate pink. Nicole smiled knowingly.

"That's between you and Kyle, honey. But remember, you're in charge. Do only what feels right."

Grace swallowed. "What feels right?" She looked down at her hands, twisting them together. "I... I want to have sex with him," she blurted out, the words rushing out like uncorked champagne. Jennifer raised an eyebrow, a slow smile spreading across her face. "Well now, there's an honest thought."

Nicole, mid-reach for a mascara wand, froze. Her hands hovered. Her pleasant smile dissolved, replaced by a look of utter, stunned disbelief. Grace? Her little girl? The quiet, sweet fifteen-year-old who treated Kyle with such innocent devotion? Her intellectual understanding of the 'temporal enhancements' David's kids inherited warred violently with the very real image of her sweet, 15-year-old daughter standing before her. It was exactly like hearing calculus come from a cartoon character.

Grace, oblivious to Nicole's internal meltdown, continued, her voice gaining a breathless intensity. "Mom, I just... I want him," she insisted, clenching her teeth, her gaze fixed on some distant, internal image. "I want to feel him... feel him pressing down, heavy and strong." She closed her eyes for a second, a shiver running through her small frame. "And I want to gasp... and feel him thrusting... inside me."

Grace opened her eyes, a fierce, determined look in them, completely bypassing her mother's state. "I want to feel him... cumming inside me," she said, her voice lower now, almost a hungry whisper. "I want to feel his hands gripping me... and feel myself... feel myself covering his cock in my own cum… repeatedly." Grace's head fell back slightly, eyes closing again as the intensity peaked. "Fuck! I can't wait!"

Nicole swayed slightly, reaching blindly for the vanity chair to steady herself. Her mouth was open, but no sound came out. She looked precisely like she'd just witnessed a squirrel quoting Shakespeare while juggling flaming chainsaws. This was NOT the vocabulary of an inexperienced teenager. This was… intense. This was… adult. This was Grace. It was a chaotic, hilarious, and utterly terrifying juxtaposition. Jennifer bit her lip, a wicked spark in her eyes. *Well, damn. Looks like I'm not the only one needing a cold shower… or perhaps a few rounds with my toys after that little show.*

Grace, finally noticing her mother's precarious state, blinked. "Oh, Mom! Relax!" she said, her tone immediately shifting back to slightly exasperated teenager. "I promised I'd wait until I'm older, you know?" She shrugged, a more familiar Grace-like gesture. "But that doesn't mean I don't have urges, Mom. Serious urges." She gave a pointed look towards the door, presumably in the direction of Kyle. "Like… really, really intense urges about my future husband."

With the makeup complete, Grace turned to the mirror, scrutinizing her reflection. The dress, the makeup, the carefully styled hair, it was all an elaborate attempt to fast-forward time, to bridge the gap between fifteen and thirty-two. She wanted desperately to be seen as Kyle's equal, to erase the awkwardness that sometimes flickered in his eyes when he looked at her.

Sophia smiled into the steamy mirror, a rare, soft curve of her lips. Tonight, she would finally go all the way with Caleb, after all, he had been so patient with her. The creak of the heavy bathroom door announced Reagan's arrival, shattering Sophia's private reverie. Reagan, all long limbs and sass, sauntered in, a towel draped carelessly over her shoulder. She tossed a knowing look at Sophia, whose cheeks were now faintly flushed.

"Big night, huh, Sophia?" Reagan drawled, propping herself against the sink, eyeing her reflection with a critical squint. "You look like you're about to confess a state secret." Sophia chuckled, a low, melodic sound uncommon for her. "Just getting ready for…date night." She finished her braid, the thick plait falling gracefully down her back. "You too?"

"Obviously" Reagan sighed, grabbing a brush and attacking her brown locks with a vigor that suggested mild exasperation. "Darrel's got some grand plan involving the new projector setup in the rec bunker, probably showing some ancient, fuzzy action movie David found. He thinks it's romantic." She rolled her eyes, but a faint, almost imperceptible smile played on her lips. Sophia watched her, a slight frown touching her brow. "You don't sound… excited."

Reagan snorted, misting her face with a floral spray. "Excited? For Darrel? Look, he's great. Really. He's handsome, he's witty, and my parents would shit a brick if they knew I was dating a black guy five years younger than me, which is a bonus. Plus, he's good to me." She paused, lowering her brush. "But it's not… you know. Not like Emma with Junior. She produces enough vaginal fuck juice to launch a cruise ship every time she's near him."

Sophia blinked, taken aback by Reagan's sudden, graphic description. "Reagan!" she whispered, half scandalized, half amused. "That's… a lot." Reagan shrugged, turning to examine her profile in the mirror. "Hey, it's just an observation. You see them together? It's like watching a volcano erupt in slow motion. All bubbling and steam and imminent, explosive discharge." She paused. "Meanwhile, Darrel and I… we're more like a friendly campfire. Pleasant. Reliable. Doesn't exactly set your knickers on fire."

She turned back to Sophia. "Makes you wonder, though, doesn't it? What's David's secret? He's got… how many wives? Nine? And they all seem genuinely, deeply obsessed with him. Like, they all look like they've just won the lottery every time he glances their way. I mean, what do you think sex with David would be like? He has to be good in bed with so many women clamoring for him."

Sophia looked away, a faint blush rising on her cheeks. She fiddled with a bottle of lotion on the vanity. "I… I've heard things." She glanced back at Reagan, her voice dropping. "I've heard that he's a very attentive and thorough lover. Like, intensely focused. Like he's made for it, almost. Every detail, every response, he just… knows."

Reagan scoffed, but a flicker of genuine curiosity crossed her face. "Attentive? Thorough? Sophia, are we talking about a lover or a goddamn mechanic giving your car a full diagnostic? That sounds kind of… clinical. Kinda boring, actually. 'Oh, David was so thorough last night, he really got into all the nooks and crannies.' Doesn't exactly explain how he's able to keep so many women satisfied. And the complete devotion! You'd think they'd get tired of being thoroughly loved." She mimed a bored sigh. "Where's the chaos? The spontaneous combustion?"

Sophia finally met Reagan's gaze, her expression unusually serious. "That's not all I heard, Reagan." Her voice was barely a whisper. "I also heard… that he can be terrifying in bed. Not in a bad way, not violent. Just… overwhelming. Intense. It's not uncommon for his wives to be bedridden the next day. Like they've been… worn out."

Reagan's jaw dropped slightly. The brush in her hand paused mid-stroke. "Bedridden?!" Her eyes widened. "Okay, now that I can wrap my head around. So it's not just thoroughness; it's thoroughness with an added side of existential dread? Like, 'I've been David-ed, and now I need a full 24-hour recovery period just to remember my own name.' Fascinating.

She lowered the brush, tapping it against the counter. "But Sophia, what kind of human being does that? We're talking about a guy who practically runs this entire operation. How does he even have the energy for that kind of… impact?" Sophia looked up, her quiet demeanor shifting to something more… knowing. "That's what I mean about 'made for it.' It's like," she searched for the right words, her gaze distant, "he has these… moods. Moments. Sometimes you just know. It's almost like a storm is brewing." Reagan leaned closer, her interest genuinely piqued now.

Sophia's cheeks blossomed with a deeper flush, but she didn't look away this time. "He'll just walk into a room, just… look at one of them. And he doesn't say anything. He just… walks over, picks them up, right over his shoulder, like they weigh nothing at all. And he just carries them away. No warning, no discussion. Just… gone."

Reagan blinked. "Over his shoulder? Like a sack of flour? And they just… go along with it?" Sophia nodded, her eyes wide with the remembered image. "They do. And then… he'll be gone for hours sometimes. And then he'll just reappear, looking perfectly normal, not a hair out of place. And then, he'll do it again. With someone else. Another wife, over-the-shoulder, and then another. I've seen it happen. He cycles through them."

Reagan slowly sat down on the edge of the large vanity, abandoning all pretense of getting ready. "He cycles through them? Like a goddamn buffet? So that's where the bedridden part comes in! I guess that would explain the 'worn out' part." She paused, a new thought striking her. "But Tiffany. She was the first, right? Before all the others. What was it like for her? Surely, with no one else, it must have been… intense."

Sophia's lips curved into a small, almost reverent smile. "Oh, it was. Tiffany… she's said it herself. Back in the beginning, when it was just her and David, she wouldn't even bother wearing underwear if it was the weekend." She lowered her voice, leaning in slightly. "She said if it was the weekend, he would… fuck her… at least eight times in a single day."

Reagan's jaw dropped, then snapped shut with a soft click. Her eyes were wide, fixed on Sophia. "Eight times? In one day? And she told you this?" She shook her head in disbelief, a slow grin spreading across her face. "Okay, now that explains a lot." She paused, a new, more intriguing thought bubbling to the surface. "Wait, so if he's like that, and his kids inherit his … whatever it is, does that, uh, extend to… that department?"

Sophia's let out a small, nervous laugh. "I… I don't know about the specifics of that," she admitted, glancing around the empty bathroom as if fearing someone might overhear. "But… I mean, you see how David is. And then you see his kids, like Junior. He's got three wives, and they're all constantly… glowing." She fanned herself lightly with one hand. "And then there's Lily."

"Lily? Oh my God," Reagan practically purred, a slow, appreciative grin spreading across her face. "That girl makes me consider switching teams faster than a New York minute. Seriously, what is in the water here?" She paused, then tilted her head, a more earnest curiosity replacing the flirtatious glint. "But seriously, Lily! And Josh? No offense to the guy, he's sweet, but Lily? How did that happen? How did he manage to snag her? Did she just trip and fall into his arms and he never let go? Because that's the only scenario I can picture where someone like her ends up with… well, I mean, he's just Josh."

"Well, it's… it's a story. And it involves Tiffany. Apparently, when Lily was like, fourteen, Tiffany took her to a livestock show." Reagan nodded. "Right, Tiffany. Makes sense. I bet she was looking at prize-winning cattle or something." She chuckled, imagining Lily, browsing the stalls. Sophia bit her lip, trying to suppress a giggle. "Well, yes, it was a livestock show. And yes, they were browsing the stalls. But… it wasn't about the animals, if you know what I mean. Tiffany has a very… proactive approach to family planning."

Reagan slowly lowered the brush, her eyebrows rising. "Oh. Oh, wow. So, it was less 'educational excursion' and more 'scouting mission'?" Sophia nodded, her eyes twinkling. "Exactly! Apparently, Tiffany had a very specific list of qualities she was looking for in a potential mate for Lily. She wanted someone strong, kind, good with his hands, and she wanted someone who would absolutely adore Lily, obviously."

"And Josh… just happened to be there?" Reagan prompted, already picturing the scene in her head. "Josh was there on a school trip from his rural county, probably looking at some prize-winning pigs," Sophia explained, her voice dropping. "And the moment he saw Lily, it was apparently P-O-W! Like a bolt of lightning. He was instantly, hopelessly smitten. Couldn't take his eyes off her."

Reagan covered her mouth, stifling a laugh. "Oh my God. So he was just… a goner from the beginning. And Tiffany just… watched?" "Oh, she did more than watch," she said, leaning closer. "She engaged him. Found out about his family, his background, his skills. Turns out he was a hard worker, responsible, and already showing promise as a country boy. So, Tiffany, being Tiffany, extended an 'invitation' for him to work on the ranch as a hand during the summers, starting that very next year."

Reagan's jaw dropped again. "No. Way. She played the long game! That's… that's genius and terrifying all at once. So, he worked here every summer, knowing Lily was here, just biding his time?" "Pretty much! But here's the kicker," Sophia added, her voice full of admiration. "Lily chose him. After a while, she saw how consistent he was, how genuinely he cared, how he treated everyone, and how devoted he was to her. So, when she turned eighteen, and David, being David, simply declared them husband and wife."

Reagan shook her head, still reeling. "That is… insane! That's some next-level matchmaking. Tiffany really is a puppet master. No wonder David trusts her to manage everything. I respect the hustle." Sophia grinned. "Exactly! Now, are you ready to go and enjoy your movie night, or do you want to hear the story of how Aidan met Alissa?" Reagan straightened up, a mischievous glint in her eyes. "Oh, we are definitely coming back to this. But first, movie night. And maybe, just maybe, I'll convince Darrel to ditch the film and tell me what he knows about this family. Wish me luck!"

Olivia bustled around the small kitchen, humming a catchy pop song to herself as she diligently finished dinner. She simultaneously packed a cooler with sandwiches, fruit, and water bottles for the beach trip. In the master bedroom, Riley flung open the closet doors, creating a small avalanche of clothing. "Okay, beach attire, engage!" she announced to the empty room. A breezy sundress here, a pair of cut-off shorts there, and, of course, her favorite oversized sunglasses.

A bright patterned bikini top was tossed into the bag, followed by a practical, yet stylish, wide-brimmed hat. She surveyed her handiwork. "Essential survival gear," she muttered, zipping the bag closed.

Meanwhile, in the smaller bedroom, a low, rhythmic thud... thud... thud reverberated within the room. Emma, who was supposedly getting ready for a shower, was pressed firmly against the plaster wall, one leg pointed straight up, creating a surprisingly sturdy brace. Her collar, was responsible for the percussive ballet, knocking against the hard surface with each relentless thrust. "N-no, Sir... not again," Emma whimpered, her voice a breathless, melodic plea. Her nails dug into his shoulder, leaving faint marks. "Fuck... I'm co-cumming again!"

Junior, a dark silhouette of focused intensity, paid her no mind. His breathing was heavy, a primal rhythm matching the insistent cadence of their joined bodies. The faint scent of their mingled arousal was thick in the air, a potent perfume of possession and absolute surrender. With a grunt that was pure, unadulterated dominance, Junior shifted. With what seemed like little more than a thought, he effortlessly spun Emma around, flipping her upside down in one seamless motion. Her leg provided a pivot point as she hung suspended, a picture of blissful, inverted vulnerability. Her whimpers turned into a high-pitched moan of shock and then, pure ecstasy.

He wasted no time. Descending with hungry precision, Junior parted her, plunging his face deep between her legs. He began to devour her, his tongue a masterful instrument of exquisite torture and pleasure. Emma's gasp was a choked sob, her fingers now clutching desperately at his thighs, attempting to capture his cock in her mouth, but failing.

"Oh… oh, Master!" she cried. Her muscles clenched around him, a violent, beautiful spasm. A wave of orgasmic bliss, raw and overwhelming, rocked her to her core. It was too much, yet never enough. Tears, hot and thick, squeezed from the corners of her eyes. She was utterly consumed, lost in the potent, all-encompassing embrace of him.

Oblivious to the seismic activity across the hall, Olivia hummed the final notes of her pop tune as she snapped the cooler lid shut. "Alrighty, that's done!" she called out cheerfully. From the master bedroom, Riley's voice floated back, a hint of impatience in it. "Is Emma ever going to get in that shower? Junior said we need to leave in… like… an hour!"

The soft click of the bedroom door opening was almost imperceptible over Olivia's cheerful humming, but Riley, sitting on their bed, caught it. Her eyes, usually sharp with sarcastic wit, widened minutely as Junior emerged carrying Emma, utterly naked and shimmering with sweat and leaking… stuff. She was cradled against him, her face buried in his neck. The soft, choked sobs Riley heard were laced with pure, raw emotion, punctuated by Emma's faint, familiar murmurs of professed adoration."

A slow, deliberate eyeroll began in Riley's mind, making its way down to physical expression. Just as she was about to call out, the bathroom door closed with a gentle click, silencing the soft lamentations of undying love. "Alrighty, that's done!" Olivia's voice chirped, the sound a stark contrast to the emotional whirlwind that had just passed. She emerged from the kitchen, a large, well-packed cooler in her arms, a bright smile gracing her lips. "Whew, snacks for days! Fruit, cheese, some jerky… oh, and those sparkling ciders Emma loves. Where is she, anyway? Need to make sure she packs her special sun lotion."

Olivia caught sight of Riley's expression, a fascinating blend of exasperation, amusement, and a touch of playful mockery. "What's wrong?" she asked, setting the cooler down with a grunt. "You look like you just saw a ghost, or… Junior and Emma being extra again?"

Chapter 9:

Date Night: At Midday

The air inside the caverns offered a refreshing contrast to the scorching Texas sun. Bonnie, her cheeks flushed with a mix of excitement and apprehension, held tightly to Seth's hand. "It's… it's just so amazing in here," she whispered, her voice echoing softly against the cave walls. A squeeze of Seth's hand punctuated her wonder. "Like a whole other world." Seth smiled; his gaze fixed on the path ahead. "It is, isn't it? Pretty special."

Bonnie took a deep breath, the cool, damp air filling her lungs. "I get it now, Seth," she confessed, her voice almost swallowed by the immense space. "Why people kiss. I understand that part." She glanced down at their intertwined hands, then back up at him, her eyes, even in the dim glow of her headlamp, shining with a bold innocence. "But… I still don't know what kissing feels like."

The silence was broken by Aidan's jovial voice. "Hey, you two! Coming?" He and Alissa stood at the entrance to a larger chamber, their headlamps casting dancing shadows on the cavern walls. Seth squeezed Bonnie's hand reassuringly. "Actually, Aidan, why don't you and Alissa go on up to the next part? We'll catch up. We've got some… important thinking to do." He kept his tone light, but his eyes held a quiet intensity as he met Bonnie's gaze.

Aidan raised an eyebrow, a slow grin spreading across his face. "Alright, lovebirds. Don't get lost in the dark!" He and Alissa turned and disappeared into the depths of the cave, their laughter a fading echo. Once alone, the silence of the cavern seemed to deepen, amplifying the sounds of their own breathing. Seth turned, gently pulling Bonnie to face him. The beam of his headlamp illuminated the smooth, ancient rock face behind her. Then, deliberately, he reached up and switched off his headlamp.

Darkness descended instantly, thick and absolute. Bonnie gasped, a small, involuntary sound. "Bonnie?" Seth's voice was a soft murmur in the blackness. "Can you feel my hand on your cheek?" She nodded, even though he couldn't see it. His thumb traced the curve of her cheekbone, a feather-light touch. "Yes," she breathed. "Okay," he said, his voice calm and steady. "Tell me what you feel, okay?" Bonnie's breath hitched. She could feel the warmth radiating from his face, sense his presence so close in the darkness. "Okay," she managed.

He shifted closer, and then she felt it, a gentle pressure, a soft warmth against her own lips. It was the lightest of touches, a mere brush. Her eyes fluttered closed. "It's… soft," she whispered, a faint blush creeping up her neck. "And… warm. But it doesn't feel anything like when we hold hands. Holding hands feels… stronger." Seth's lips lingered, a whisper against hers. He didn't press further. "What about now? With them touching like this?" he asked, his voice a soft caress in the darkness.

Bonnie instinctively tightened her grip on Seth's shirt, her fingers digging into the fabric. His breath ghosted across her lips, a fleeting touch that sent a jolt of nervous energy through her. Then, in a reflexive act, her tongue flicked out, a tiny, nervous exploration. It met his lips, a fleeting, wet contact.

She jolted back slightly, a surprised gasp escaping her. "Oh! I... I licked you," she stammered, her voice high-pitched with embarrassment. "It's okay, Bonnie. That happens. You don't have to be embarrassed." Their lips still touching, a tentative connection in the inky blackness, he asked again, "What do you feel now?"

Bonnie's senses were reeling. The initial surprise had faded, replaced by a curious, almost electric tingling. It was a confusing mix of sensations, both amplified and muted. The coolness of the cavern air seemed to disappear, and all she could focus on was the gentle pressure of Seth's lips. "I... I think my legs are gone," she murmured, her voice thick with wonder and a touch of disbelief. "I can't feel them anymore." Seth's smile was evident in the slight shift of his lips against hers. "That's good, right?" he whispered.

Bonnie managed a shaky nod. And then, a mischievous thought, a bolder impulse, bloomed in her mind. She wanted to kiss him. Taking a deep breath, she leaned forward again. This time, she didn't hesitate. She met his lips, and as their mouths connected, she felt a surge of something akin to triumph. But in her eagerness, her approach, a little too enthusiastic. Her lips closed around his, and with a soft, wet sound, she accidentally sucked in a small portion of his lower lip.

A tiny, surprised gasp escaped Seth. Bonnie froze, a hot flush of mortification creeping up her neck. But the mortification was quickly swallowed by an irrepressible giggle, a tinkling sound that seemed to bounce off the ancient rock formations. It was absurd, delightful, and undeniably hers. Driven by the sheer, bewildering joy of it all, her tongue darted out, a bolder, more exploratory sweep this time, meeting his.

It was different now, a shared exploration, a silent conversation happening in the vast, subterranean emptiness. Her head buzzed, not unpleasantly, with the thrum of their mingled breaths and the slick, warm glide of their tongues. It was… gross, maybe? But the only thing Bonnie could think, the only sensation that dominated her reeling senses, was the overwhelming, undeniable truth: she wanted more. Much, much more. How could something so weird feel so… electric?

A voice cut through the delicious, awkward haze. "Seth? Bonnie? You guys good back there?" Aidan's voice, slightly muffled by distance and rock, echoed down the tunnel. Bonnie flinched, pulling back from Seth as if struck by a spotlight. A fresh wave of heat flooded her face. He heard something? Or maybe she was just paranoid. She suddenly felt like a giant, clumsy kid who'd just been caught with her hand in the cookie jar, except the cookie jar was Seth's mouth and her hand... well, her whole face.

"Yeah! Yeah, Aidan!" Seth's voice was a little higher than usual, a slight crack betraying his own surprise. He sounded just as flustered, which somehow made Bonnie feel a tiny bit better, and then instantly worse. Was she that bad at it? Was her tongue thing weird? She probably looked ridiculous in the dark. "Alright, alright, just checking," Aidan chuckled. "Getting a little too quiet back there. Alissa was starting to think you two had found a secret passage to India or something."

Seth clicked his own headlamp on. The sudden wash of light felt blindingly bright, revealing the small pocket of cavern they occupied. Seth blinked, his eyes adjusting, and his cheeks were definitely flushed. Bonnie felt like she was under a microscope. She instinctively smoothed her hair, then her shirt, like that would somehow erase the past thirty seconds. Did he see? Could he tell? Was my mouth open too wide? Was it slobbery? Oh god, the tongue thing... She felt a wave of mortification wash over her, cold despite the lingering heat in her face. She was such a kid. He probably thought she was awful at it. Totally clumsy.

"Coming!" Seth called out, taking a step forward, and Bonnie followed automatically, keeping her headlamp beam pointed vaguely at the ground. They shuffled down the narrow passage towards the main tunnel where Aidan and Alissa waited. He cleared his throat quietly. "So... uh... how did that... feel?" Bonnie nearly tripped. How did it feel? Like a chaotic, messy, mortifying disaster. "Um," she managed, her voice small. She risked a quick glance up. "It was... different?" she mumbled, which felt like the understatement of the century. God, she was bad at this. "I kind of… I think I did it wrong."

Seth stopped, gently pulling her to a halt in the narrow passage. "Wrong?" he repeated. There was a hint of confusion, maybe even disappointment, in his voice. Bonnie yanked her gaze back to the ground. "Yeah. Like… I dunno. My tongue felt weird. I'm sorry. I guess I'm just… not very good at it."

A beat of silence stretched between them. Bonnie braced herself for the inevitable, the moment he'd realize just how awkward and clumsy she was and regret the whole idea. Then Seth chuckled softly. It wasn't a mean sound, more like surprised warmth. "You think you did it wrong?" he asked, his grip tightening slightly on her hand. He stepped a little closer, and she could feel the faint warmth radiating from him. "Because if it was so 'wrong'… then why do I… really want to do it again?"

Bonnie's head snapped up. Her eyes met his, wide in the gloom. The sincerity in his expression, the way his eyes crinkled slightly at the corners even in the dim light, stole her breath. He wanted to do it again? After that? The mortification didn't vanish, but it suddenly had to share space with a blossoming, surprising warmth that spread down from her chest to her fingertips. She swallowed, the words catching in her throat. It felt terrifying and exhilarating all at once. Keeping her hand firmly clasped in his, she finally managed to whisper, "Me too."

Inside the master bedroom, a softer, much more engaging heat was brewing. David leaned into a kiss with

Jessica. Her petite frame fit against his perfectly, and her sassy, sarcastic wit was the tonic to his often-serious mind. Jessica pulled back, a mischievous look in her eyes. "Are we going to watch the movie, or are you hoping for a pre-show?" she teased, her voice a low purr.

David chuckled. "Patience, little one. The anticipation is half the fun." He released her, watching as she turned towards the walk-in closet. "Oh, I have plenty of patience," Jessica retorted, her back to him as she began to shed her light dress. "It's you I'm worried about. You're practically vibrating with… husbandly enthusiasm." David grinned, running a hand over his head. He loved the way she challenged him, even as she adored him. She was already naked, her silhouette framed by the gentle light filtering in from the window. As she reached for a fresh top, a soft, oversized shirt she often wore for their indoor evenings, David moved.

He approached her from behind, silent as a shadow, and wrapped his arms around her naked body. His chin rested on her shoulder, and he inhaled the scent of her, clean and faintly floral. Jessica shivered, a delicious reaction he knew well. "What was that about patience, Daddy?" David murmured, his lips brushing the sensitive skin below her ear. Jessica sighed, leaning back into his embrace, her hands coming up to meet his. "You're incorrigible," she whispered, her sarcasm a thin veil over genuine affection. "And it's 'movie night.' We have an audience waiting." "Our audience can wait another five minutes," David countered, pulling her closer, feeling the curve of her spine against his chest.

Jessica turned in his arms, her large breasts brushing against his chest. She wrapped her arms around his neck, pulling him down for a kiss. It was a slow, sensual kiss, filled with promise and unspoken desires. "I'm sure," she whispered against his lips. "I need this. I need you." David didn't need to be told twice. He lifted her effortlessly, her legs wrapping around his waist. He carried her towards the bed, his eyes locked on hers. "Then let's make the most of these five minutes," he said, a wicked glint in his eyes.

After lowering her down, she promptly sat up, taking his cock in her mouth. David let out a surprised, pleased groan, his hands instinctively going to cup her head, his fingers tangling in her soft hair. Jessica, ever the instigator, hadn't wasted a single second of their self-imposed 'five minutes.' Her eagerness was a powerful aphrodisiac, a testament to the unique connection they shared, a bond forged not just in affection, but in a profound, almost intellectual understanding of what made the other tick.

"Well, now," David chuckled, his voice a little strained, a tremor running through him as she worked her magic. "Someone's certainly keen on pre-show entertainment." The warmth of her mouth, the skillful precision of her movements, sent waves of intense pleasure through him. For all his intellectual prowess, moments like these, he was entirely at her mercy. A delicious irony.

He leaned back slightly, his eyes half-closed, enjoying the view. Her posture was artful, almost reverent, but the glint in her eyes told a different story, one of mischievous intent and fierce possession. Her full breasts swayed gently with her movements, a tantalizing distraction. She knows exactly what she's doing, he thought, a familiar appreciation for her sharp mind and playful spirit washing over him. And she knows exactly how to make me forget everything else.

David's fingers traced the delicate curve of her spine, marveling at the strength and agility hidden beneath her seemingly delicate frame. Her scent, a heady mix of vanilla and something uniquely 'Jessica', spicy and sweet, filled his senses, clouding his mind. He bit back another groan, his body arching slightly into her ministrations. The urge to thrust, to claim her completely, was a primal roar in his ears, battling against the refined control he usually prided himself on. Even with all his control, this woman had a way of bringing him undone with just a look, a touch, or, as now, the exquisite dance of her tongue.

Jessica, sensing his rising intensity, only pressed on, a low, playful hum vibrating from her throat. Her eyes, wide and sparkling with mischief, flickered up at him from beneath a curtain of blonde hair, a silent dare in their depths. She knew exactly how close he was to the edge, and she relished every tremor that ran through his powerful frame. The rhythmic suction, the way her lips teased the base of him, the firm, knowing press of her palate, it was a symphony of sensation designed to push him to his absolute limit. He felt the blood rush from his head, pooling in a throbbing inferno between his legs.

With a sudden surge of strength, born of pure desire, David scooped her up, her small frame surprisingly light in his hands. He hoisted her, legs now resting easily on his broad

hands went to his head, clutching softly as she returned the kiss with an eager hunger that belied her recent exhaustion. It was an affirmation, a conversation spoken without words, reinforcing the deep, primal bond between them.

When they finally broke apart, it was with a soft pop, a thin strand of saliva stretching between their lips before snapping. It was a messy, intimate detail that only served to heighten the raw sensuality of the moment. Jessica's breath hitched, her eyes now wide open, burning with a renewed fire. Jessica wiped his mouth with her hand, a small smile playing on his lips. "Well, that was certainly… thorough."

Jessica's chest heaved, her heart still thrumming. Her voice, when it came, was a little breathless, but laced with her characteristic sass. "Thorough? Daddy, you practically siphoned my soul out through my clit. And I'm not complaining, mind you." She paused, her gaze dropping to his mouth, then lower, a predatory gleam entering her eyes. "But now," she declared, her voice dropping to a low growl, "you've got me all primed and ready. I'm vibrating, Daddy. And I need you to do the rest. I need you to fuck me. Right here. Right now."

With a quickness and a determination that almost deemed impatient and delightfully frustrated, she grabbed his cock, guiding it inside of her. David met her urgency with a deep, rumbling sound in his chest, a sound of pleasure and approval. Jessica, true to her word, was a delightful vibratory mess, a live-wire of raw need. Her hips began a ferocious cadence, the bed springs groaning a rhythmic protest that was quickly drowned out by her soft gasps and the slick sounds of flesh meeting flesh. Each thrust was an exclamation point to her earlier declaration, a furious, primal demand that David was more than happy to answer.

His hands, broad and knowing, cupped the impressive weight of her breasts, his thumbs circling the areolas before his mouth latched onto a hardened nipple. He sucked deeply, a slow, deliberate drawing that sent shivers through her spine, making her arch into him even harder. Jessica's head fell back, a blissful groan escaping her lips as David's tongue swirled around the engorged peak, teasing and tasting. "Impatient, Baby girl?" David murmured against her skin. He pulled on her nipple gently, eliciting a sharp, sweet cry from her. "Just… getting… started, Daddy!" she panted, her voice tight with pleasure. Her eyes, still half-lidded, met his, burning with an unyielding intensity. She wasn't just bucking; she was grinding, twisting, trying to bury him inside her completely.

David chuckled. "Oh, I can tell." He released one nipple only to capture the other, his free hand sliding down to cup her ass, lifting her slightly, adjusting the angle for deeper penetration. He began to thrust with her, slow at first, mirroring her initial rhythm, then steadily building, a controlled power that perfectly matched her escalating frenzy. He could feel every twitch, every shiver, every subtle shift in her tight embrace, and he responded with a precision that bordered on art. Jessica cried out as he hit a particularly sensitive spot, her knuckles white as she gripped his shoulders. "There! Right there, Daddy! More!"

He obliged, leaning in to whisper against her ear, his breath hot against her skin. "As you wish, my delicious little slut." His words were a silken rope, pulling her deeper into his rhythm, deeper into the maelstrom of sensation they were creating. The room seemed to fade, replaced by the symphony of their shared desire: the creak of the bed, the wet sounds of their coupling, Jessica's impassioned pleas, and David's low, encouraging murmurs.

Jessica bucked against him, her breathing ragged. "Oh, God, Daddy... I'm so close..." her voice was a strained whisper, a plea. David, his own breathing deepening, slowed his pace just a fraction. He cupped her face, lightly pinching her cheeks, forcing her to meet his gaze. His eyes, usually so calm and analytical, were now blazing with a primal intensity. "Not yet, Baby. Hold on a little bit longer. Savor it." A playful glint sparked in his eyes, the witty David momentarily resurfacing amidst the raw passion. "Besides, what kind of 'Daddy' would I be if I let you off the hook so easily?" He punctuated his words with a deep, teasing thrust, making her gasp.

Jessica groaned, her body trembling with the effort. "Sir, please... I can't... It's too much..." She whimpered, her nails digging slightly into his chest. The pleasure was so intense it was almost painful, a delicious torment she both craved and feared. David continued his deliberate pace, withholding. He knew exactly how to walk that razor's edge, pushing her right to the brink without letting her fall. The sweat glistening on her forehead, the frantic look in her eyes, it all fueled his own desire, sharpened his focus. He was so close to exploding.

Just as his control threatened to snap, just as the world began to narrow to the pulsing heat between them, Jessica cried out, her voice filled with desperate urgency. "Daddy, please! I need to cum!" David, caught in the tidal wave of his own impending climax, hesitated for a heartbeat. He looked down at her, at the raw vulnerability etched on her face, the pure, unadulterated need that mirrored his own. He couldn't deny her. With a guttural groan that vibrated through her very core, he released the reins, abandoning himself to the moment. He gave one final, earth-shattering thrust as he finally allowed himself to come, and simultaneously he whispered, "Come for me, baby. Come now."

Jessica's body exploded. A primal scream tore from her throat as wave after wave of intense pleasure washed over her. Her muscles clenched around him, milking him dry as she rode the crest of her own orgasm. She felt like she was flying, weightless and free, lost in the blissful oblivion of pure sensation. Her vision blurred, and she clung to him desperately, afraid she might simply dissolve into the ether, nearly fainting from the experience alone.

Jessica's breath hitched, a soft, contented sigh escaping her lips as she lay draped across David, her body still humming from the aftershocks. His cock, though softening, still throbbed gently inside her, a warm, reassuring weight. The last tremors had faded, leaving her delightfully boneless, her face buried in the crook of his neck. "Mmmph… just five minutes," she mumbled, her voice muffled against his skin, sounding entirely too satisfied to move.

David chuckled. He ran a gentle hand over her back, tracing the curve of her spine, feeling the lingering tremors beneath her skin. "Five more minutes, my little queen of sloth?" he murmured, a hint of playful mockery in his tone. "I seem to recall a certain petite, sassy woman agreeing to a date night in the Rec bunker, starring a movie tonight. And if I'm not mistaken, the sun is still quite high.

Meanwhile, in the cool, artificially lit tunnel, Grace hummed softly to herself. Her heart fluttered with a nervous excitement she usually reserved for a really good scout mission. Tonight, however, her target was Kyle, and the mission was romance. As she ascended the first steps into the apartment bunker's main stairwell, she spotted Lynn heading in the opposite direction. Lynn, catching sight of Grace, stopped dead in her tracks. Her eyes widened, scanning Grace from her perfectly styled hair to the hem of her elegant dress. A small gasp escaped her lips, quickly followed by a disbelieving chuckle. "Grace! My word! Is that really you?" Lynn stepped closer, a grin spreading across her face. "You look… stunning! Absolutely stunning! I almost didn't recognize you. That dress, that hair… you look five years older, at least!"

Grace blushed, a shy smile touching her lips, but a spark of newfound confidence shone in her eyes. "Thank you, Lynn! You look nice too, by the way," she added, genuinely. Lynn, still beaming, lightly clapped her hands together. "Well, I should hope so, it is date night, isn't it? For you, anyway!" She winked good-naturedly. "Are you off to Kyle's apartment?" Grace nodded, her cheeks warming further.

"Yes, dinner. The kitchen is providing meals." She imagined Kyle, probably waiting, perhaps polishing a firearm or two, completely oblivious to the transformation awaiting him. She couldn't wait to see his face. She'd made sure to arrive just on time, not a minute early.

"Well, you go on then, sweetheart," Lynn said, stepping aside to let Grace pass through the stairwell archway. Her expression held a knowing sparkle. "Have a wonderful time. And, uh, good luck!" Grace giggled softly, the "good luck" hanging in the air with a playful double meaning. "Thanks, Lynn! You too!" she called back, already turning to head towards Kyle's door. She heard Lynn's soft laughter fading behind her as she continued her journey, a new spring in her step.

Chapter 10:

Date Night: The Afternoon

The rhythmic rapping echoed in the sterile hallway, a nervous flutter in Grace's stomach amplifying the sound. She was nervous, a feeling she wasn't quite expecting, but the implications of date night settled on her like snowflakes. The door swung inward, revealing Kyle, clad in a simple grey t-shirt and jeans. His jaw practically unhinged as his eyes landed on Grace. He blinked, then blinked again, as if trying to clear his vision. His mouth worked, but for a moment, no words came out.

"Wow..." Kyle finally managed. He ran a hand through his messy, dark hair, his gaze sweeping over her from head to toe. "Grace? Is that... you?" He took a hesitant step back, as if afraid she was a figment of his imagination that would disappear if he got too close. He was expecting Grace for dinner, but he didn't expect her to look so nice. Grace offered a shy smile, her cheeks flushing a deeper shade of pink. "Hi, Darling," she said softly. "Surprise?" She held up the insulated bag containing their dinner. "I brought the food. Figured you'd be hungry."

Kyle continued to stare, his brain clearly struggling to reconcile the girl he knew with the young woman standing before him. The soft, floral dress, the expertly applied makeup, the way her hair was styled...it was all so different, so…grown-up. Grace looked stunning. Breathtaking, even. It was a bit overwhelming, and…dare he admit it? Intimidating.

"Right. Uh… come in, come in," Kyle stammered, finally stepping fully aside, a hand still raking through his hair. Grace stepped inside, her keen eyes immediately sweeping over the main living area. The usual scattered schematics, cleaning kits, and firearm components were conspicuously absent. The counter tops gleamed, and even the cushions on his worn armchair looked plumped and orderly. A faint scent of citrus cleaner hung in the air, replacing the familiar metallic tang of gun oil.

Grace's shy smile widened into a genuine, delighted grin. Her eyes sparkled as she turned back to him, a playful glint dancing in them. "Kyle! You cleaned!" she exclaimed, her voice laced with an affectionate teasing. "It's… immaculate. I almost didn't recognize the place. Did you hire a team of miniature fairies?" She gestured around with an exaggerated sweep of her hand.

Kyle's cheeks flushed a deeper crimson than the subtle blush on her own. He rubbed the back of his neck, suddenly finding the polished floor fascinating. "Well, you know… date night," he mumbled, sounding a little like a teenager caught doing something embarrassing. "Figured it should be, you know, presentable." He cleared his throat, trying to regain some semblance of his usual composure. "Uh, just put the food down on the counter.

Grace giggled, enjoying his flustered state immensely. It was exactly the reaction she'd hoped for, proving her efforts hadn't gone unnoticed. She walked over to the small, functional kitchen counter, carefully placing the insulated bag down. The comforting aroma of roast chicken and herbs wafted out, a testament to the main kitchen's expertise. As Kyle took a tentative step towards her, perhaps to grab the bag, Grace moved with the swift, almost stealthy grace she possessed. Before he could fully react, she spun, taking a quick step forward and throwing her arms around his neck. She launched herself slightly, rising onto the balls of her feet, and pressed her lips firmly against his.

The kiss was deep, confident, and utterly unexpected. Kyle stiffened for a microsecond, his mind blanking once more. He'd kissed Grace before, but this… this was different. This was a woman kissing him, with an intensity that stole his breath and sent a jolt straight through him. Grace, ever so observant even in the moment, shifted her head slightly, angling just so to ensure her carefully applied lipstick remained perfectly intact. She pulled away slowly, a soft, satisfied sigh escaping her lips, her eyes still closed for a beat before fluttering open.

When they did, they met Kyle's wide, dazed gaze. His arms, which had instinctively come up to steady her as she launched herself, were now loosely around her waist, holding her close. He looked utterly undone. His messy hair seemed even messier, and his jaw was still slightly agape. "Better?" Grace whispered, her voice laced with amusement and a touch of genuine affection. She leaned her forehead against his chest, listening to the rapid thump-thump-thump of his heart against her ear.

Kyle blinked, the question finally registering through the haze of surprise and… something else. His grip on her waist, which had tightened almost imperceptibly, eased just enough for him to nod, a single, jerky motion. "Uh… yeah. Better," he managed, his voice a little hoarse. He cleared his throat, his ears still ringing from the unexpected depth of the kiss. He glanced down at her, then back up at the insulated bag on the counter, as if trying to re-establish the sequence of events.

Grace, ever perceptive, saw the wheels turning in his head. She pushed off him gently, giving him space, but not too much. "Good," she hummed, turning towards the counter. "Now, let's get this feast sorted. The main kitchen outdid themselves tonight." She moved with an easy grace, pulling out the carefully packed containers. Roasted chicken, fragrant with rosemary and garlic, golden potatoes, and steamed green beans spilled their warmth into the apartment. Kyle watched her, still a little stunned, but a faint, appreciative smile started to form on his lips as the delicious aromas filled the air.

Grace laid the plates out with meticulous care, then returned to the counter for the chicken. She brought the serving platter closer to Kyle's side of the table first. "Men should always be served first, don't you think?" she chirped, her voice innocent, even as she leaned over him, her body nearly touching his as she scooped a generous portion onto his plate. As she pulled back, her hand brushed his arm, and she paused, tipping his head up to press a chaste, yet firm, kiss to his lips. "Hope you're hungry."

Once she was settled in her seat, Grace smiled, a glint of something unreadable in her eyes. "So, Kyle," she began, her voice serious. "Things are starting to get… stable here. The generators are humming, the crops are growing, David's got it all under control. But what about… later? When things really start to get back to normal? Do you ever think about leaving the ranch?" She paused, giving him a chance to answer. "Going back to the old world, maybe? Building a life somewhere else? Or are you planning on sticking around here for the long haul?"

Kyle paused mid-chew, his fork hovering over the plate. He swallowed, his mind suddenly racing. The question caught him completely off guard. Leaving the ranch? He hadn't really considered it. The ranch was safe, secure, a little weird, but comfortable. Before the CME had destroyed everything, that was his goal, just to be comfortable. To settle in a comfortable rhythm.

"Leaving?" he finally managed, the word a little rough around the edges. He took a sip of water, buying himself a few more seconds. "Grace, that's… that's a big thought. I mean, look around." He gestured vaguely with his head. "We've got everything here. Power, water, food for years, all secured. David's made this place a fortress. And my work…" He gestured towards the closed door. "It's not exactly easy to pack up a whole armory, a forge, and everything else I need, and just… set up somewhere new, you know?"

He chuckled, a short, slightly nervous sound. "Before all this," he continued, trying to sound nonchalant, "my biggest worry was finding a place to run my business. Now,

I'm building custom rifles and training people how to defend themselves. This is… important work. And I like it. I like the rhythm of things here. I like knowing that what I do matters, that it keeps us all safe."

He met her gaze, a small, genuine smile forming on his lips. "And honestly, Grace, I haven't really given it a second thought. The old world… it's gone, isn't it? What's to go back to? A bunch of abandoned cities and empty promises? This is home now. This is where we're building something new, something real." He paused, then, remembering his manners, added, "But what about you? Is that something you've been thinking about? Returning to… whatever was before?"

Grace sighed softly, swirling the remaining water in her glass. "It's not that I want to go back to before," Grace explained, "It's that I worry about the ranch getting too crowded. As families grow, will there be enough space? Will everything be alright? It's something that keeps me up at night." As Kyle ate, Grace reached for a bottle of wine.

Grace uncorked the bottle with a practiced ease that made Kyle blink. He watched, fascinated and a little alarmed, as she poured a respectable amount into his glass, then her own. He opened his mouth, a protest already forming on his lips. But before a single syllable escaped, Grace fixed him with a look. It wasn't angry, or even stern, but it was incredibly… adult. And it was clear: Don't even think about it, Kyle. He snapped his mouth shut.

He swallowed, suddenly feeling like he was the one being lectured. This wasn't the Grace he remembered. This was… an entirely different caliber of young woman. The floral dress, tailored perfectly to her developing frame, the subtle makeup that highlighted her eyes, the poise with which she held her wine glass, it was all designed to make him forget her age, and it was working disturbingly well. He felt a flush creep up his neck. This is going to be a long night, isn't it?

Meanwhile, in Caleb's room, Sophia and Caleb had abandoned their video game and were already on his bed making out. The soft sounds still chirped from the console, a forgotten relic of their previous activity. Sophia had reached over, paused the game, and without a word, leaned in to kiss Caleb. He hadn't hesitated, his fingers immediately dropping the controller to cup her face, pulling her closer. Now, tangled in the blankets, her soft brown hair fanned out on the pillow, Sophia giggled softly as Caleb trailed kisses along her jawline. "Hey," she whispered, her voice teasing, her hands tracing the line of his spine. "You said you were going to beat my high score."

Caleb pulled back just enough to grin, his eyes sparkling. "Plans changed," he said, tucking a loose strand of hair behind her ear. "This is way better." He kissed her again, deeper this time, a contented sigh escaping him. Worries about the ranch's future, about space, about anything beyond the warmth of her body against his, were miles away.

As their kisses deepened, a new current entered the intimate dance. Sophia's fingers, which had been tracing patterns on his back, subtly but purposefully shifted. Her hands intertwined with his, gently guiding them from his waist, beneath the hem of her simple t-shirt. The soft fabric rode up, and then his palms were pressed against the warm skin of her lower back, a soft intake of breath escaping her lips. He felt the delicate curve of her spine, the subtle swell of her hips beneath his touch. It was a silent invitation, a silent permission, and Caleb's heart hammered a little faster.

He moved his thumbs in slow, circular motions, savoring the feeling, but he hesitated, his gaze seeking hers. Despite the rising heat between them, he was acutely aware of the line, the unspoken boundaries. She shifted, a theatrical sigh escaping her. "Ugh, this is getting ridiculous," she murmured, her voice a playful complaint. "My pants," she gestured vaguely at the denim clinging to her legs, "they keep getting all... tangled in the bedding. It's really uncomfortable," she paused, her gaze dropping pointedly to where their bodies were pressed together.

Caleb's eyes widened, a slow grin spreading across his face. "Oh, really? Tangled, huh?" He mimicked her tone, playful and suggestive. "That is a problem. We wouldn't want you to be uncomfortable. Not at all." Sophia's lips twitched, fighting back a smile. "Exactly. If I'm going to be stuck in your room all night," she emphasized those last few words with a mischievous raise of her eyebrows, "we might as well get comfortable."

Without breaking eye contact, Sophia swung her legs off the bed and stood up. She turned her back to Caleb, unbuttoning the top button of her jeans, then slowly sliding down the zipper. The sound was surprisingly loud in the small room, amplified by the sudden quiet that had fallen between them. With a final tug, the jeans slid down her hips and pooled around her ankles. She stepped out of them, a slight sway to her hips, and turned back to face Caleb, a confident smirk playing on her lips.

He hadn't been prepared for this. He'd imagined the kiss, the touch, the slow build-up of intimacy, but he hadn't pictured this. Standing before him, illuminated by the soft glow of the LCD screen 'window,' Sophia was breathtaking. Her simple t-shirt clung to her curves, and beneath it, peeking out from the top, he could just make out the lace trim of a bralette. But it was her lower half that had him completely captivated.

Gone were the bathing suits and ever-present practical shorts he was used to seeing her in. Instead, she wore a pair of simple cotton panties in a soft shade of lavender. He'd never seen her in anything like them. They were… surprisingly innocent, yet undeniably alluring. The soft fabric hugged her hips, the elastic waistband sitting low on her stomach. He noted the smooth curve of her thighs, the delicate dip of her waist. It was a completely different side of Sophia, a softer, more vulnerable side than he'd ever witnessed.

Sophia seemed to be entirely in control of her faculties, which, given her usually quiet demeanor, was an impressive feat. She took a slow, deliberate step towards the bed, her eyes still locked on his. Then, a small, mischievous smile played on her lips, a tiny spark of daring in her usually demure gaze. "Your turn, cowboy," she murmured. "Lose the pants. I don't want your belt or any of those fiddly metal bits snagging on my skin." Her eyes dropped pointedly to his waist, then back up to meet his.

The command, blunt and direct despite her soft tone, jolted him back to reality. Or, at least, to the primal instinct of immediate obedience. His hands flew to his belt buckle, fumbling with it as if it were a complex alien puzzle. The metallic clink sounded like a gunshot in the hushed room. He unzipped his jeans with a speed that would impress a drag racer, his heart pounding a frantic rhythm against his ribs. Pants off. Immediately. So immediately, in fact, that he didn't even bother to fold them or place them neatly. They simply collapsed in a heap around his ankles, looking like a discarded pile of denim shame. He stepped out of them, nearly tripping over the crumpled fabric, and stood there in his boxer briefs, feeling both ridiculously exposed and utterly triumphant.

Sophia's smile widened just a fraction, a silent acknowledgment of his hasty compliance. She shifted on the bed, making room for him. As Caleb slid back onto the mattress, closer now, her warmth instantly enveloped him. He could feel the soft, almost imperceptible brush of goosebumps rising on her legs against his own, a delicate electricity that ran through him.

Then, as she nestled deeper into him, her head resting on his shoulder, a new sensation filled his awareness. It wasn't a perfume, or soap, or anything artificial. It was a faint, earthy, subtly sweet scent, unmistakably her. It was the scent of feminine arousal, a soft, intoxicating musk that seemed to deepen with every beat of his heart. "You smell nice," he blurted out, the words escaping before his brain could filter them. It wasn't quite what he'd meant to say, but given his current state of sensory overload, it felt like a profound observation.

As they continued making out on his bed, a delightful, dizzying haze settled over Caleb's mind. His brain, usually a whirring engine of anxieties and plans for the next shift, had effectively shut down, replaced by a single, overriding directive: more of this. He felt a soft, almost imperceptible pressure on his thighs, then the gentle weight as she hooked a leg around him. A moment later, she was straddling him, her body radiating a different kind of heat, a focused, intense warmth that bypassed his boxer briefs entirely and went straight for his core.

Spurred by a sudden, overwhelming urge to have her even closer, Caleb's hands, which had been resting vaguely on her back, tightened. He pulled her close, his arms wrapping around her waist, the action almost involuntary. Her body weight settled fully onto him, pressing him deeper into the mattress with a satisfying thud. It was a sweet, heavy surrender, a complete intertwining of their forms that made his lungs feel delightfully squashed. He could feel the delicate curve of her hips against his, the soft swell of her belly, the subtle shift of her breasts against his chest.

Sophia, apparently unfazed by his sudden bear hug, simply nestled deeper, her face burying itself in the crook of his neck. Her hands, previously tangled in his hair or tracing lazy patterns on his back, now took a more decisive turn. Her delicate fingers took one of his larger, clumsier hands and guided it. Under the hem of her shirt it went, a soft whisper of fabric against the back of his hand. He felt the smooth skin of her lower back, then the delicate curve of her spine. It was exhilarating. Like discovering a secret map to buried treasure, and Sophia was the one holding the compass.

Her fingers continued to guide his, a silent, knowing instruction that bypassed all need for words. Upwards they went, a slow, deliberate ascent. And then, his fingers brushed against something new. Fabric, yes, but different. A strap. A hook. The distinct feel of lace and elastic. His brain, which had been functioning on a very basic, primal level, finally registered the location. The middle of her back. Her bra.

Caleb's internal monologue screamed. This is it! The moment of truth! But… how does this thing work? He glanced at Sophia, her eyes closed, a small smile playing on her lips. She clearly expected him to know what to do. The pressure was immense. He was pretty sure he'd seen it done in a movie once, but he couldn't remember which one. Deciding against playing it cool, he opted for practicality. With both hands, he unclasped her bra, freeing her breasts. The action wasn't exactly graceful. More like a startled lobster attacking a rubber band. Sophia let out a breath as her breast fell free from their previous state.

Before Caleb could even process the full glory of the view, or figure out if he was supposed to keep his hands there or reverently withdraw them, Sophia, with a surprisingly fluid movement, did something entirely unexpected. One arm snaked up, unconcerned with his hands, and grabbed the hem of her top. In one swift, graceful motion, she peeled it upwards, taking the unfastened bra with it. The soft fabric whispered over her head, and for a glorious, fleeting second, Caleb was treated to the full, unadulterated sight of her.

With a quick smile, she pulled his head up to her breasts, clearly inviting him to taste them. The soft, warm weight of Sophia's breasts against his mouth was an immediate, overwhelming sensation. Caleb, his brain still buffering from the bra incident, reacted on pure instinct. His lips parted, a gasp escaping him that was immediately muffled by luscious skin. He latched onto a nipple, a hesitant suckle, then another, a little more confident. It was soft, firm, and astonishingly... there. His eyes, wide with a mix of surprise and dawning understanding, closed as he focused entirely on the tender, exhilarating taste.

His hands, still hovering uselessly, now found a purpose. One instinctively moved to cup the side of her breast, supporting the weight, while the other traced a path along her ribcage, feeling the soft curve of her waist. A low, contented hum vibrated from Sophia, and Caleb felt a sudden surge of pride. He was... doing it right? Maybe? This whole 'first time' thing was a lot less about grand gestures and a lot more about figuring it out on the fly.

He was so utterly consumed by the delightful new experience that Sophia's next move caught him completely off guard. With a subtle undulation of her hips, she shifted minutely, and then, a warm, soft hand, surprisingly deft and firm, ghosted over his lower abdomen. His eyes flew open, but he couldn't even process what was happening before her fingers, cool against the heat of his skin, reached down. There was a gentle tug, a distinct rustle of fabric, and then, a sudden, glorious release.

His breath hitched. He wasn't sure if it was the surprise, the freeing sensation, or the realization that she had just, without a word, reached into his boxer briefs and pulled his dick, already straining, into the open air. The cool air on his suddenly exposed skin was a shock, quickly replaced by the soft pressure of her fingers, wrapping around him. Caleb nearly inhaled an entire breast. His internal monologue, already a chaotic symphony, reached a crescendo. She just… she just did that! Oh god, it's out. It's really out. And she's… touching it. He looked up, his voice a strained whisper. "Are… are we going to do this?" Sophia didn't say a word. She simply bit her lip, looked him in the eyes, and nodded.

Meanwhile, beneath the ranch house, the movie was already started, its fantastical landscape of puppets and practical effects filling the massive screen in the opulent Recreational Bunker. The air-conditioning hummed, a slight contrast to the warm air typically surrounding the pool. The massive screen was capturing the projected movie in the dark. Darrel and Reagan were seated on two of the reclining chairs, legs intertwined, already a symphony of whispered jokes. Across from them, Josh and Lily shared another chair, Lily practically glued to Josh's side, her hand resting possessively on his thigh.

David, with Jessica in tow, tried to make a quiet entrance. Jessica, holding a large brown bag of popcorn that threatened to burst at the seams, pointed to two seats in the middle of the makeshift theater. "Daddy, those look comfy," she chirped, her eyes twinkling. David nodded, placing a gentle hand on the small of her back. Darrel spotted them and couldn't resist. "Looks like someone had a long pre-show," he quipped, a sly grin spreading across his face. Reagan giggled, nudging him playfully. "Seriously, David, you're late for your own movie! Did you get lost on the way down?"

David chuckled. "Traffic was a bitch," he replied, a hint of amusement in his voice. Jessica giggled, blushing slightly as she elbowed David gently. "Daddy!" she whispered, fighting back a grin. Josh, oblivious to the subtext, chimed in, "Yeah, David, what kept you? They're already at the bog of eternal stench." Lily, ever the quick-witted pragmatist, leaned in close to Josh, her lips brushing his ear. "It's Dad," she whispered, her voice low and laced with a knowing amusement. "You know damn well where he was."

Just then, a small commotion erupted near the entrance. Jennifer, Summer, and Nicole arrived, their arms laden with various containers. "Sorry we're late!" Jennifer called out, her voice carrying through the bunker. "We were putting the finishing touches on the dinner date meals." "Hope you saved us some seats!" Summer added, scanning the available recliners. David beamed at the trio, his gaze lingering on each of them for a moment. He gestured to the adjacent recliners. "Ladies, perfect timing. And thank you, all three of you, for making tonight so special. Your support for date night means the world to me."

Nicole set a couple of containers near Darrel and Josh before finding a seat. But Jennifer, instead of taking a seat, immediately dropped to her knees in front of David. A collective but quiet gasp swept through the bunker. Jennifer lowered the neckline of her top, revealing her breasts with confident abandon. Then, reached for the button of David's pants, a determined look in her eyes. "Jennifer!" Jessica squealed, swatting Jennifer's hand away with surprising force. "There are other people here!" She blushed furiously, glancing around at the stunned faces. Darrel's jaw was practically on the floor.

Jennifer, her face a mask of mortification that warred with a flicker of defiance, scrambled back to her feet. "Right! Sorry!" she stammered, pulling her shirt up to cover herself, though the gesture felt a little late. "It's… suddenly quite chilly in here." She hurried towards the stairs, her retreating form a flurry of embarrassed energy. "Just going to grab a throw. My room. Really just… need a blanket." Her voice trailed off as she disappeared around the corner.

David's lips twitched, a well-suppressed chuckle escaping him. He caught Jessica's eye. "Well," he drawled, "that escalated quickly." Reagan leaned in closer to Darrel, her voice a low murmur that only he could catch. "She's not cold, Darrel," she whispered, a smirk playing on her lips. "She's getting a throw blanket to cover herself while she gives David either a handjob or a blowjob."

Darrel, struggling to reconcile what happened, began to ponder. He thought about David's children, their exceptional abilities. Grace's perceived youth, and his wives' beauty. "Maybe it's all connected," he muttered to himself. "Maybe David's DNA really is the key." The soft, ethereal glow from the projection cast shifting shadows on Darrel's face as he mumbled, lost in thought. Reagan, her head tilted, caught a few of his stray words. "What was that?" she whispered back, nudging him lightly with her elbow.

Darrel leaned closer, his voice dropping to a near inaudible whisper, eyes wide with a mix of genuine curiosity and the dawning realization of how absolutely insane his theory sounded. "Reagan," he began, glancing quickly at Josh and Lily who were engrossed in the film, and then at David and his other wives, huddled comfortably together. "You know how they say David's children inherit his... skills and all that?" Reagan nodded slowly, her smirk returning. "Yeah, the whole maturity gene thing?"

Darrel leaned closer. "What if it's... more? What if it's not just the knowledge, but... everything? His wives, they all look so damn good, right? And smart. Super smart." He paused, taking a breath, before finally spitting it out. "Do you think... do you think David's... cum... makes his wives youthful and smarter?" Reagan stared at him in the dim light, a beat of silence passing as the Goblin King's face filled the screen behind them. Then, a quiet snort escaped her, quickly stifled. "Darrel," she managed, her voice thick with amusement, "you're seriously asking me if David's semen is some kind of magical anti-aging, brain-boosting elixir?"

Darrel's eyes darted around, checking if anyone was listening, before leaning even further into Reagan's space. "Think about it, Reagan! They're all trying to get it, aren't they? Like Jennifer, just now! And David... he's... pumping them full of it from both ends, like some kind of daily vitamin!" His whisper had grown more urgent, his logic, however flawed, building in his own mind. "Grace, right? She's what, fifteen? But what of she's not? What if she's as old as he is?"

He gestured wildly, albeit subtly, towards the couch where David was nestled between Jessica and Summer, Nicole nearby. "It's not just David's smarts and good looks they're after, Reagan. It's the fountain of youth! The fountain of knowledge! It's like a biological download every time! He's literally impregnating them with wisdom and anti-aging properties!" Darrel finished, a triumphant, if utterly bewildered, look on his face.

Reagan clamped a hand over her mouth, her shoulders shaking with silent laughter. Her eyes, wide and sparkling in the dim light, were fixed on Darrel's earnest face. A tear slipped from the corner of her eye. "Darrel," she finally choked out, pulling her hand away, her voice a strained whisper, "Are you suggesting David's... seed... is like, a superfood smoothie for women? And that's why they're all so eager for a 'David-dose'?" A fresh giggle escaped her, a little louder this time.

Reagan broke, her laughter echoing in the Rec Bunker. Heads turned, David's included, but the Goblin King's musical number held their attention. Darrel, panicked, knelt beside her, trying to stifle her mirth-induced convulsions. "Shhh! Reagan, you're gonna blow my cover! He'll know we're onto him!" he hissed, waving his hands frantically. "Maybe he'll force us to drink some of his juice!"

Reagan managed to gasp for air, tears streaming down her face. "His... juice?" she sputtered, the phrase sending her into another fit of giggles. "Oh, Darrel, you're killing me!" From the couch, Jessica, ever observant, raised a perfectly sculpted eyebrow. "Everything alright over there?" she called out, her voice laced with amusement. David simply chuckled, shaking his head slightly.

Chapter 11:

Date Night: The Evening

Suddenly, the bunker door swung open, and Jennifer breezed in, a fluffy throw blanket clutched in her arms. She surveyed the room, her gaze lingering on David before squeezing between him and Summer. "Mind if I sit here?" she asked, flashing a playful smile. Reagan, stifling another giggle, nudged Darrel. "Oh, this is going to be good," she whispered. Jennifer settled in, carefully arranging the blanket over her legs. Summer offered her a polite smile, while David simply raised an eyebrow in silent question. Jennifer batted her eyelashes innocently. "Just a little chilly," she chirped. Darrel, however, was having none of it. He watched with rapt attention, mentally preparing a detailed report for Caleb and Noah later that night.

The credits rolled on, and a comfortable silence settled over the bunker. The air was thick with the scent of popcorn and anticipation for the next film, "Dan in Real Life." Josh, ever the curious boy, looked back to David, a puzzled furrow in his brow. "David, what's this one about? Never heard of it." David chuckled. "It's a funny romcom, Josh. A little bit awkward, a little bit sweet. You'll enjoy it."

As the opening scenes unfolded, Darrel fidgeted in his seat, still buzzing from his ridiculous discovery. The "David's semen equals super-intelligence" theory had taken root in his mind, and he couldn't shake the feeling that he was witnessing some kind of bizarre, marital superpower at play. He glanced at Jessica, who was practically glued to David's side, a contented smile on her face. Was it love? Or was it... something else? He made a mental note to add "observe Jessica's behavior" to his ever-growing list of research topics.

The soft, romantic melodies of the soundtrack filled the air. Josh was still engrossed, laughing at the early awkward encounters between the characters. Darrel, however, wasn't paying attention at all. It had started subtly, a faint, almost imperceptible hum. Everyone in the dark theater, from Nicole to Lily, and even Darrel himself, had instinctively reached for their pockets, fumbling for non-existent cell phones. A few mumbled, "Not mine," or "Must be the generators," before shrugging and returning their attention to the movie. But the hum persisted, a low, rhythmic thrumming that seemed to emanate from the very air around David's section of couches. It was less a buzz of technology and more... a contented drone.

Darrel, still half-convinced he was an amateur sociologist observing David's unique domestic ecosystem, tuned in with heightened focus. He watched as David, who had been leaning slightly to accommodate Jennifer's sudden, blanket-clad arrival, now looked even more strained. Jessica remained blissfully asleep, her head nestled against David's arm, a soft, almost imperceptible snore occasionally punctuating the film's dialogue. But Jennifer... Jennifer was no longer merely 'squeezed between.' She was very deliberately, very comfortably, nestled directly in David's lap, the fluffy throw blanket, which now seemed less an indicator of chilliness and more a strategic camouflage, spread neatly over both of them.

David, a seasoned veteran of navigating his wives' affectionate machinations, was trying to lean around Jennifer's head to get a clear view of the screen. His head was cocked at an unnatural angle, one arm still supporting the sleeping Jessica, the other subtly trying to brace himself against the armrest without disturbing Jennifer. The faint buzzing sound, Darrel now realized with a jolt, was coming from Jennifer. Or rather, through Jennifer. Darrel nudged Reagan again, this time with an urgent jab of his elbow. "Reagan," he whispered, his voice a frantic hiss, "Do you hear that? The... the hum?"

Reagan, initially engrossed in the film, frowned, pulling one earbud out. "Hum? Like... electricity? Should we be worried? Aidan said he fixed th-" "No, no, not the generator! Listen!" Darrel practically vibrated with nervous excitement. He leaned closer to Reagan, his eyes wide. "It's... it's coming from Jennifer!" Reagan rolled her eyes, a familiar expression of exasperation flickering across her face. "Darrel, you're being ridiculous. Maybe it's her stomach?" "No, no, it's rhythmic. And... and it's getting stronger." Darrel pointed a trembling finger towards Jennifer. "Look at her face, Reagan! She's... she's making faces! "

Reagan, despite her initial skepticism, reluctantly shifted her gaze from the screen to Jennifer. She squinted, focusing on the woman nestled so intimately in David's lap. And that's when she saw it. Jennifer's normally expressive face was contorted in a series of subtle, almost imperceptible twitches. Her lips were slightly parted, her eyes half-closed, and a faint flush was creeping up her neck. "Holy Fuck!" Reagan breathed, her initial amusement quickly morphing into dawning realization. "You're right! What the hell is she doing?"

Darrel leaned in even closer. "I don't know! Is she… is she fucking him right there? Under the blanket? Or is she squatting on… you know… a vibrator?" He gestured vaguely downwards with his hand, his face a mixture of shock and morbid fascination. Reagan stared at Jennifer, then at David, who still seemed oblivious to the internal combustion engine purring in his lap, then back at Jennifer again. "I think…" she said slowly, a mischievous glint sparking in her eyes, "I think it's both, Darrel. I think they're both getting buzzed."

She snorted with laughter, earning a few glares from Summer and Nicole, who were actually invested in Dan's romantic struggles. "They're sharing the experience!" Reagan managed to choke out between giggles. Darrel's jaw dropped. "No way! You think David's… immune to the buzz? He's just sitting there like it's nothing?"

Reagan, still trying to stifle her giggles, shook her head, a new thought dawning on her. "Immune? Darrel, this is David we're talking about." Her eyes drifted over the assembled group, a quick mental count of David's many wives flicking through her mind. "Sophia was so right," she muttered. "He really does have a lot of sex. Like, a lot a lot. Even with this many wives, he still finds time for… this." Her gaze settled back on David, who was now subtly shifting his weight, his arm casually draped around Jennifer's waist, almost imperceptibly drawing her closer.

"What was that?" Darrel whispered, leaning in again, his eyes glued to the blanket-shrouded scene on David's lap. "Nothing," Reagan replied, but her eyes narrowed, suddenly captivated. She'd initially thought David was just... David, content and oblivious. But now, as the dim light from the screen flickered across his profile, she caught it. A shadow of a smile, not just content, but something else. Something... cunning. Almost sadistic. It was so faint, so fleeting, that she questioned if she'd imagined it.

Her amusement morphed into fascination. This wasn't just Jennifer getting off on his lap; this was a performance, a shared secret between them, and David was clearly the conductor. The thought sent a shiver down her spine, not of fear, but of sheer, unadulterated curiosity. What was he planning? What was his move going to be? He certainly wasn't just "immune to the buzz." He was a predator, a puppet master, and Jennifer was his willing, purring instrument.

Reagan leaned back slightly in her seat, trying to look casual, but every fiber of her being was now hyper-focused on David. She wanted to see it. Whatever "it" was. She wanted to witness the next stage of this silent, public display of marital... intensity. She wanted to see David's grand masterplan unfold. "Look at him," she breathed, nudging Darrel lightly. "He's not doing nothing." Darrel's eyes darted from Jennifer's still-twitching form, barely visible beneath the blanket, to David's oddly serene face. "What do you mean?" he murmured, clearly still processing the initial revelation.

"He looks like he's just… watching the movie. Like he's bored."

Reagan snorted under her breath. "Bored? Darrel, that man is never bored. Look at his eyes. He's plotting." She leaned closer, her voice dropping to an urgent whisper. "He's doing something to her now. Something… deliciously wicked." Just as Darrel was about to respond, a sharp, choked yelp cut through the movie's soundtrack. It was Jennifer. She tried to cover her mouth, clearly attempting to stifle the noise, but her body betrayed her. She lurched, convulsing violently, falling forward onto the seat in front of her, the blanket slipping to reveal her shaking body.

A collective gasp went through the rows. Josh paused mid-popcorn munch, his eyes widening. Lily, sitting beside him, tensed, looking concerned. Jessica, startled from her sleep, shot a look at Jennifer, a hand flying to her mouth. Summer and Nicole just shook their heads. Then came the sound. It started subtly, a muffled gurgle, then rapidly escalated. A loud, wet slosh-slosh-splish echoed through the theater, like someone had just poured a bottle of water onto the floor. It was unmistakably… intense.

Jennifer, her body still wracked with shudders, finally collapsed. Her knees buckled completely, and she slid off David's lap, down to the floor in front of him, a small, shimmering puddle expanding beneath her. She lay there, face-down, twitching, a soft, spent groan escaping her lips. David, meanwhile, remained utterly unperturbed. He just reached down, casually, and draped the blanket more completely over Jennifer's prone form, then returned his gaze to the screen, a faint, almost imperceptible smirk growing on his face.

Darrel stared, from Jennifer's trembling body to David's nonchalant face. "Holy... holy shit, Reagan," he finally managed, his voice a strangled whisper. "You were right. He is a wizard. And I think... I think she just... flooded the place." "Flooded the place," Reagan breathed, a slow smile spreading across her face. It started small, a tremor of disbelief, then bloomed into genuine, unadulterated awe. Her jaw, which had been slack, now firmed. "Oh my God, Darrel. You maniac. I think you were right."

Josh, still holding his half-eaten popcorn, exchanged a bewildered look with Lily. "Is... is she okay?" Josh mumbled, leaning forward slightly, though not daring to move from his seat. Jessica, who had recovered from her initial shock, let out a soft snort. "Oh, she's more than okay, Josh. She's just been properly Mastered." Her eyes twinkled with a mixture of amusement and a hint of nostalgia. "It happens. Not always quite like a geyser, but... you get the picture." Summer just continued to shake her head. "Serves you right, you nasty whore," she said before throwing a piece of popcorn into her mouth.

The air in Caleb's room was thick with the aftermath of... well, aftermath. Sophia lay nestled beside Caleb, her dark hair splayed across the pillow, a faint blush still on her cheeks. Caleb, propped up on one elbow, was blowing on her exposed chest, attempting to dry the sweat. "That was...

amazing, Sophia. Seriously. Amazing." Sophia smiled shyly. "It was… nice." Caleb grinned. "Nice? That was way beyond nice. That was…earth-shattering." His grin faded slightly. "Hey, uh, how many of those… you know… condoms… did you bring?" Sophia blinked. "I think… maybe enough? Why?"

Caleb shifted, suddenly looking a little flustered. "Well… um… because I kind of want to do it again." He avoided her gaze, fiddling with a loose thread on the blanket. "Is that weird? I mean, was it okay for you? I don't want to rush you or anything…" Just then, a knock sounded on the door. Not a gentle tap, but a distinct, almost impatient rap. "Caleb? You in there, man? It's Darrel!" Darrel's voice, muffled but clearly audible, carried through the wood.

Caleb groaned, rolling his eyes as he pulled the blanket higher. "Go away, Darrel! I'm busy!" he called out, his voice a little strained. He hadn't expected anyone to come looking for him, especially not now. He exchanged an exasperated look with Sophia, who was trying to stifle a giggle. A moment of silence, then another, softer knock. This time, a female voice, distinctly Reagan's, followed. "Sophia? Are you in there with Caleb?"

Caleb's eyes widened, a fresh wave of panic washing over him. "Reagan?!" he whispered, aghast, to Sophia. "How does she know you're in here?" He scrambled to cover himself, pulling the sheet up to his chin, his previous fluster replaced by genuine shock. Sophia, putting on a loose t-shirt, simply rolled her eyes. She pulled the door open just enough for a peek, but Darrel and Reagan, propelled by an almost manic energy, didn't wait for an invitation. They burst into the small room, their faces flushed from what looked like a mixture of excitement and utter bewilderment.

Caleb, still halfway under the blanket and looking embarrassed, let out a strangled gasp. He pulled the sheet higher, practically burying himself. "Dude! Give us a second!" Darrel, however, was already pacing the tiny carpeted space, running a hand through his hair. His eyes were wide, a manic gleam in them. "A second?! Caleb, man, you won't believe what just happened downstairs! I'm telling you, it's gotta be the semen! It just has to be!"

Reagan, looking a little more composed, leaned against the doorframe. "Darrel, calm down. You're scaring them." She then gave Sophia a knowing look and a small, apologetic shrug. "Hey, Sophia. Sorry to interrupt, but Darrel's about to spontaneously combust if he doesn't tell someone." "Spontaneously combust? Reagan, Jennifer almost spontaneously combusted!" Darrel exclaimed, stopping his pacing to fix Caleb with an intense gaze. "You know how David's wives are always... eager? Well, I have this theory about his, you know, jizz making them look younger and smarter?" Caleb groaned from under the covers. "Darrel, this is not the time for your... theories."

"It is the time, man! It's the only time!" Darrel insisted, practically vibrating. "We were all watching a movie downstairs. But then, Jennifer... she was sitting there on David's lap, and David was next to her, just watching the movie like she wasn't there." Reagan picked up the story, a slight shiver running down her spine despite herself. "Then

Jennifer started, you know, wincing a bit. And we kinda noticed David smiling, which still seemed… innocent. Until it wasn't."

Darrel slapped his thigh, his eyes widening further. "Dude, I think he had his dick out the whole time! And she was riding a vibrator with his dick inside her! Right there! On the couch! While we were watching a movie!" His voice dropped to a conspiratorial whisper, as if the walls themselves might be listening. "And then… then he did something. I don't know what, but it was like… a trigger!" Sophia blinked, her earlier amusement fading slightly into genuine shock. "Wait, what?"

"She yelped!" Reagan chimed in, equally flabbergasted. "Not like a little yelp, either. Like a full-blown, 'fuck I'm cumming' kinda scream! And then… oh my god, I'm never going to forget it…" Darrel finished with a flourish, his eyes wide in disbelief. "She just… exploded! Her own cum, man, she just keeled over, pouring cum on the floor. And then… poof! She just… passed out. Out cold! On the floor!"

As Darrel delivered his final, explosive pronouncement, his gaze, finally, drifted past the foot of the bed, past the rumpled sheets, and landed directly on Sophia and Caleb, who were now staring back at him, wide-eyed. A beat of charged silence hung in the air, thick enough to cut with a dull knife. Darrel's mouth, still open from his dramatic conclusion, slowly closed. His eyes, initially burning with the shared trauma of the movie-theater incident, now widened even further, a slow flush creeping up his neck. Reagan, following his gaze, simply shook her head, smiling.

"Oh," Darrel managed, his voice barely a squeak. His enthusiasm, which had fueled his entire recounting, deflated like a punctured balloon. "Oh, my bad. So… you guys were… getting some." He gestured vaguely at the sheets, then at them. Caleb, ever-calm, let out a slow, deliberate breath. "Yeah, Darrel. You could say that." A nervous energy crackled in the tiny room. "Well, congratulations, man!" He slapped Caleb on the shoulder harder than necessary.

He turned to Sophia, face bright red. "And you, Sophia! Looking after my boy Caleb. He mumbled a quick, "Have fun! Be safe!" and then stumbled out of the room, dragging Reagan behind him. As the door clicked shut, the silence returned, this time only broken by the slightly muted chuckles of Caleb and Sophia. "Well," Caleb said. "That was… unexpected." Meanwhile, right outside the door, Darrel stopped dead in his tracks, slapping his forehead. "I am such an idiot! I just cock blocked my man Caleb! What is wrong with me?"

Reagan chuckled, shaking her head. "You're just excited, babe. I think they figured that out." Darrel sighed. "Man, everybody be fuckin' up in this place!" he said as he turned to leave. Sophia froze, her shirt, caught in her arms over her head. Her face, which had been a soft flush, deepened to a fiery crimson. She slowly turned to Caleb, a look of incredulous mortification on her face. Her brow furrowed, a silent plea for him to explain, to make sense of the sheer awkwardness that had just enveloped their private moment.

Caleb, still chuckling, slowly stepped out of the bed and walked toward her. "Don't worry," he murmured, his voice laced with amusement. "He means well. Just… enthusiastic." He reached out, wrapping his arms around her. "And maybe a little too loud." "Enthusiastic is one word for it," Sophia whispered, dropping the shirt to the ground. "I think he's trying to live vicariously through us." Caleb chuckled, nuzzling her neck. "Maybe. You know, we don't have to let one loudmouth ruin our evening."

On the highway, Aidan gripped the steering wheel of his beast. Alissa sitting beside him, her hand resting on his thigh. In the back, Seth fiddled with Bonnie's ring, while Bonnie stared out the window, lost in thought. "So," Aidan said, breaking the comfortable silence. "Caverns were… interesting." Alissa laughed. "That's one word for it. It was scary there without lights and guides."

Seth leaned forward. "It was cool, though! The formations, the echoes… and the pools of water." Bonnie remained quiet, a small smile playing on her lips. Aidan glanced in the rearview mirror, catching her eye. "You okay back there, Bon?" he asked. "You've been awfully quiet." Bonnie blushed. "Yeah, I'm fine. Just… thinking." "Thinking about what?" Alissa prompted gently. "Nothing," Bonnie mumbled, then blurted out, "The caverns were… romantic."

Aidan and Alissa exchanged a quick, knowing glance, a shared smile passing between them. Alissa leaned back in her seat, eyes twinkling. "Romantic, huh? What exactly made it so romantic, Bonnie? Bonnie's blush deepened, if that were even possible. She risked a quick peek at Seth, who was now fidgeting with his own hands, though a faint, proud smirk tugged at the corner of his mouth. Aidan chuckled, glancing at Seth. "Come on, Seth, Bon. Spill it. Something clearly happened in the dark. Did Seth try to hold your hand in the dark? Trip and fall into a romantic embrace?" he teased, pulling the words from them slowly.

Seth puffed out his chest slightly, a wide, innocent grin spreading across his face. "Well, we... we kissed!" Aidan nearly choked on air, letting out a dramatic gasp that made the car momentarily swerve. "You what?" he exclaimed, feigning shock. "Seth, you smooth operator! In a cave? That's next-level romance, kid." He glanced at Alissa, who was already stifling giggles. Alissa put a hand over her mouth, her shoulders shaking with laughter. "Oh, Bonnie! That's wonderful! Is that why you were so quiet? Did you enjoy it?"

Bonnie nodded shyly. "Yeah. It was... nice," she murmured. Her gaze flickered to Seth, then down to her lap. Alissa caught the subtle shift. "Just 'nice,' Bon?" she prompted softly, her tone warm and encouraging. "No fireworks? No violins playing? Or was there something... a little different about it?" Bonnie squirmed, picking at a loose thread on her sleeve. "Well, it was... wet." She mumbled, almost inaudibly. "And... and a bit messy. I think I... I licked him. And then he licked me back. And then we just... licked each other." The last part came out in a rush, a mix of embarrassment and genuine confusion.

Aidan, who had been listening with an amused smirk, let out a startled chuckle before catching himself. He quickly coughed to cover it, but his shoulders were still shaking. "Licked each other, huh?" he repeated, a grin threatening to crack his composure. "So, uh, how exactly did that happen? Was it like a... full-on face lick? Or just the lips?" He tried to sound serious, but a mischievous twinkle danced in his eyes.

Before Bonnie could even formulate a response, Seth, who had been listening intently with growing alarm, suddenly straightened up. "Aidan!" he blurted out, a little more loudly than he intended. "Don't be weird! It wasn't like that! It was... it was a proper French kiss!" He glanced at Bonnie, his expression softening considerably. "And Bonnie... she's a really good kisser, actually. It wasn't messy or anything. It was..." He trailed off, searching for the right words, "It was perfect."

Bonnie's head shot up, her eyes wide with surprise. "A French kiss?" she repeated, the confusion slowly morphing into something akin to relief. "Seriously? I thought... I thought I did it wrong. It felt so... clumsy." Alissa laughed. "Clumsy for your first time, maybe, but absolutely right! It's all about connection, about exploring. It gets smoother with practice, I promise you." She glanced at Aidan, a knowing look passing between them. "Good save, Seth," she commented, then turned her full attention back to the younger pair, her smile warm. "But the real question isn't how it happened, or even if it was 'proper', though Seth clearly thought it was," she teased. "The real question is, did you two really enjoy it? Be honest now. Both of you."

Seth nodded vigorously, his cheeks flushed. "I did! It was… it was amazing." He looked at Bonnie expectantly. Bonnie fidgeted with the hem of her dress, a blush creeping up her neck. After a long moment, she mumbled, "Yeah. It was… okay." Aidan raised an eyebrow. "Okay, huh? Just okay?" Alissa pressed gently. "Or perhaps… better than okay?" Bonnie's head snapped up, her eyes sparkling with a mixture of embarrassment and excitement. She took a deep breath, suddenly emboldened. "It was… it was more than okay. Actually," she confessed, her voice gaining strength with each word, "I want to do it again. Like, really want to do it again. Like, right now."

Aidan took a moment to process the sheer audacity of Bonnie's statement. "Alright, alright, hold your horses there," he drawled. "I'm not saying I wouldn't turn a blind eye if you two decided to, you know, go at it again. But I do feel it's my civic duty to warn you about the perils of excessive immediate contact." "You see," Aidan continued, oblivious to Alissa's silent protest, "too much vigorous kissing, especially when one is particularly enthusiastic, can lead to 'lip rub burn.' It's a real thing. Chafing. Discomfort. Nobody wants that on a date night. You gotta pace yourselves. You don't want to peak too early. Metaphorically speaking, of course."

Seth let out a mortified groan, clapping a hand over his face. Bonnie, however, looked less embarrassed and more intensely curious. She blinked. "Lip rub burn?" she repeated, testing the words. "Is that like… a blister?" Alissa intervened, stifling a laugh. "It's more like subtle carpet burn on your chin and face, can be painful." She then looked directly at Bonnie.

202

"Believe it or not, Aidan and I were actually around your age when we first met. He was 15, I was 13. And let me tell you." She leaned in slightly, as if sharing a profound secret, "I had to wait a full two years before I even got my first real kiss from this one." She gestured playfully at Aidan, who merely shrugged, a hint of sheepishness in his eyes.

Bonnie's eyes widened. "Two years?" she breathed, looking from Aidan to Alissa, a sense of awe mixing with surprise. "But... you two are married now. How did you... wait?" Alissa chuckled, reaching out to squeeze Aidan's hand. "Well, it wasn't exactly easy," she admitted. "You have to remember, things were different back then. I was living with my mom in Tucson. My dad was... well, let's just say he had a knack for finding trouble. Elena, being the amazing aunt she is, decided I needed a change of scenery. So, she brought me here to Texas when they moved here, two years later."

Aidan interjected. "We were pretty much smitten right away, so we spent those two years chatting on the phone nonstop. Then we moved to Texas. And that first week, we definitely made up for lost time." "In fact," Alissa added, a nostalgic smile playing on her lips, "we kissed so much that first week, I ended up with such a bad case of 'lip rub burn', as my charming husband here so eloquently put it, that I had to wear a truly hideous bandage on my chin for like, a week straight. It was not my most fashionable moment."

"So, 'lip rub burn'..." Bonnie mused, her voice dropping to a serious, almost scientific tone. "It's like... you have to be very careful with the lips? Like a... delicate operation?" She looked from Alissa to Aidan, then back to

Alissa, her brow furrowed in concentration. "So, when we kissed, was that... too much?" She pointed a hesitant finger at her own lips, then at Seth's, a look of dawning horror on her face. "Did I give you lip rub burn, Seth? Oh no!"

Seth, a little flustered by Bonnie's sudden outburst, stammered, "N-no! Bonnie, you didn't give me 'lip rub burn'. It was... it was very gentle. We were being careful, right?" He looked to Aidan for reassurance. Aidan, suppressing a grin, chuckled. "He's right, Bonnie. You're fine. Lip rub burn is more of a... professional hazard," he added, smiling at Alissa. Alissa lightly slapped his arm. "Don't scare the children, Aidan! But seriously, Bonnie, Seth is right. As long as you're not scrubbing each other's faces together like you're trying to remove freckles, you should be alright."

Bonnie's face cleared, relief washing over her. "Oh! So just... gentle. Got it." A pause. Then, her eyes lit up with an impish glint. "So... can we kiss some more?" "H-here?" he stammered, his eyes darting quickly from Bonnie's eager face to the rearview mirror, where Aidan and Alissa were trying, and failing, to hide their amusement. "You mean... right now? In the car?" Bonnie nodded enthusiastically, her eyes wide and sparkling like a mischievous sprite. "Yeah! What's wrong with here? It's dark in the back, and we can't see much anyway." She gestured vaguely at the windows.

He hadn't even managed to string together a coherent thought before Bonnie, armed with new knowledge, was tugging him closer. "Wait, Bonnie," he squeaked, but it was too late. Bonnie was a woman on a mission. Aidan and Alissa were practically vibrating with suppressed laughter in the front seats, but Bonnie ignored them completely. She cupped Seth's face in her hands, her expression intense, and then she kissed him. Not a tentative peck, but a full-on, exploratory kiss.

Seth froze for a split second, then his instincts took over. He closed his eyes, abandoning himself to the moment. He fumbled a little, unsure how to respond, but Bonnie, surprisingly, seemed to know exactly what she was doing. And then… the tongue. It was just a feather-light tracing at first, the tip of Bonnie's tongue dancing along the edge of his lower lip. Seth's heart hammered against his ribs. This wasn't the shy girl from several hours ago. He felt his mouth part slightly, a silent invitation, or maybe just pure shock.

Bonnie didn't hesitate. With a delicate slide, her tongue entered his mouth. It was a quick, soft exploration, a gentle dance that sent shivers down his spine. He felt his arms automatically wrap around her waist, pulling her closer. The car suddenly felt very small, very warm, and very… intimate. A long moment passed, time blurring into a single, electric sensation. Finally, Bonnie pulled away, breaking the connection. A strand of saliva stretched between their lips for a tantalizing second before snapping. Seth gasped for air, his cheeks flushed, his eyes wide and dazed. "Wow," he breathed, the word barely audible. Bonnie grinned, looking utterly pleased with herself. "So? Was that gentle enough?"

Chapter 12:

Date Night: The Night

The iconic "FIGHT!" boomed from the speakers. Grace, despite her earlier poise, morphed into a whirlwind of button-mashing, her fingers flying across the controller with surprising ferocity. Her Sonya Blade moved with an almost unhinged grace, landing combos that seemed more by divine intervention than actual skill. Kyle, on the other hand, was a picture of focused concentration, meticulously planning his moves with his Liu Kang. "Seriously, Grace?" Kyle exclaimed, dodging a wild kick. "Are you just mashing every button at once? That's not a strategy, that's a panic attack!"

"It's called 'fluid improvisation,' Kyle dear," Grace retorted, her eyes glued to the screen, a triumphant grin spreading across her face as Sonya landed a devastating bicycle kick. "And sometimes, chaos is the most effective weapon against predictable 'tactical brilliance'!" The first round ended with a decisive "FATALITY!" from Grace's Sonya, leaving Kyle's Liu Kang a crumpled, pixelated mess.

The triumphant ding of the round win reverberated through Kyle's apartment, punctuated by Grace's cackle. She leaned back against the plush cushions of the sofa, a wine glass precariously balanced in one hand, controller still clutched in the other, her floral dress, a little rumpled from her fervent gaming. Kyle, however, merely stared at the pixelated remains of Liu Kang, a single eyebrow raised in disbelief. "A panic attack, Grace. That's what that was. Pure, distilled panic." He took a sip. "One lucky hit, maybe two. You flailed your way to victory."

"Oh, is that what it was?" Grace challenged, her eyes twinkling mischievously. "Because I distinctly recall a 'FINISH HIM!' and your humble monk doing a rather dramatic face-plant. Perhaps your 'tactical brilliance' just couldn't keep up with my… 'unconventional' methods." She wiggled her eyebrows, leaning in closer. "Don't tell me, darling, are you intimidated by a woman who doesn't adhere to your rigid combat doctrines?"

Kyle chuckled, shaking his head. "Intimidated? Never. Amused? Always. Alright, round two. Let's see if chaos theory holds up under pressure." He restarted the game, the familiar character select screen popping up. "Still Sonya?" "Always Sonya," Grace affirmed, her lips pursed in concentration as she selected her fighter. "She understands the beauty of an unexpected knee to the face."

This time, Kyle managed to hold his own for longer, even managing a few impressive combos, but Grace's Sonya, like a digital phoenix, kept rising from the brink of defeat. Finally, with a triumphant cry, Grace landed a brutal leg grab, followed by another "FATALITY!" prompt. Kyle groaned dramatically as Liu Kang was unceremoniously dismembered on screen. "I call hacks," he said, setting his controller down with a mock sigh of defeat. "That's it. I'm taking a shower."

Grace beamed, setting her controller down too. "It's called skill, my love," she teased from the couch. Kyle smirked, getting up from the floor. "Flattery won't get you a rematch." As he passed the couch, Grace swiftly executed a well-timed leg trap, her floral dress bunched, revealing more of Grace's toned legs as she twisted, deftly hooking Kyle's ankle with her own. He stumbled, a surprised laugh escaping him as he pitched forward, catching himself on her shoulders. Her face, still flushed from the wine and the thrill of victory, tilted up, her mischievous eyes locking onto his.

"Oh, but maybe this will get me a rematch," she whispered, her voice a low, playful challenge, already thick with the easy intimacy building. Before Kyle could retort, Grace surged up, pulling him closer. Her lips found his, soft and sweet at first, a gentle press that tasted faintly of the Cabernet they'd shared. Then, emboldened by the moment, the kiss deepened, a slow, sensual exploration that made the air in the small apartment crackle.

When they finally broke apart, both a little breathless, Grace's eyes were sparkling. She leaned back, still nestled in his embrace, a triumphant smile playing on her lips. "I think that merits at least a re-evaluation of my skills, wouldn't you agree?" Kyle chuckled, running a thumb over her cheekbone, smudging a tiny bit of the expertly applied eyeshadow. "Re-evaluation, perhaps. Rematch? Still debating. But I will say," he leaned in, pressing a soft kiss to her forehead, "your 'skill' is quite persuasive." Grace giggled, a carefree sound that filled the apartment. "Good. Because I need a shower too."

She hopped off the couch, the mature dress suddenly feeling far too constricting. "You go ahead, mister," she said, waggling her eyebrows. "I'll... be right back." Kyle chuckled, shaking his head at her playful antics. He turned and headed towards his bathroom, already peeling off his shirt. As soon as the door clicked shut, Grace's carefree demeanor evaporated, replaced by a focused determination. Her eyes darted to the closed bathroom door, confirming Kyle was safely ensconced. A quick, almost imperceptible smirk touched her lips. She snatched the empty Cabernet bottle from the table. Her bare feet made almost no sound on the carpet as she padded swiftly, silently, out of Kyle's apartment.

She reached Junior's door, inserting her own keycard into the slot, unlocking the door instantly. Grace moved with the stealth of a ninja, her eyes immediately scanning for the kitchen. She bypassed the living area, heading straight for the sleek, well-stocked refrigerator. Her fingers danced over the cold metal, a quick search locating what she needed: another, unopened bottle of the same Cabernet from the main kitchen's generous supply. Perfect. She took the bottle, placing the new one delicately on the counter, then, with a silent clink, deposited the empty bottle into Junior's unsuspecting trash bin.

Mission accomplished on the wine front, Grace made a beeline for the bathroom. The thought of the warm spray, the scented soaps, was truly appealing after the excitement of the evening. She stripped off the dress, letting it fall in a silken pool on the tiled floor. Stepping into the shower, she let the warm water cascade over her, washing away the slight stickiness of the wine, the lingering scent of dinner, and any last vestiges of the teenage facade she still sometimes wore. She savored the moment, a silent laugh bubbling up inside her.

After a quick, invigorating shower, Grace emerged, removing the shower cap and toweling her body dry with one of Junior's plush towels. She glanced at her dress, still a crumpled heap, then back at the mirror. Her eyes, still sparkling, met her reflection. A sly, confident smile spread across her lips. Gathering her now-damp dress in one arm, and the fresh, unopened bottle of wine in the other, Grace tied the towel securely around her. She slipped out of Junior's apartment as quietly as she'd entered, the door clicking softly behind her.

Grace let herself back into Kyle's apartment. The cool glass of the wine bottle felt like a trophy against her arm as she deposited her now-damp dress on the chair beside the door. The distinct whoosh of water from the bathroom was still strong, a comforting white noise that confirmed her window of opportunity was still wide open. She uncorked the new bottle of Cabernet, the soft pop a mere whisper in the quiet space. The rich, ruby liquid flowed steadily, refilling both her and Kyle's glasses, topping them off to a generous level. She replaced the cork in the new bottle, setting it beside the gleaming glasses.

Next, a quick detour to Kyle's closet. The door swung open silently, revealing a neat row of shirts, their fabrics, a mix of soft cottons and sturdy blends. Her fingers ghosted across them, settling on a charcoal grey t-shirt, soft, worn, and smelling faintly of him. It was oversized, perfect. A mischievous grin tugged at the corners of her lips as she glanced down at the towel still cinched around her body.

With a shrug that was more liberation than effort, the towel slipped to the floor with a muted whisper. The cool air of the apartment kissed her skin, a sudden, exhilarating rush. She stood there for a heartbeat, starkly, undeniably naked. Her gaze drifted to Kyle's bed, a large, inviting expanse of rumpled sheets and pillows. A wave of warmth, not just from the residual wine, bloomed in her chest. Lying there, just like this, felt… right. Like a declaration. Like something a person who was already married would do.

The satin sheets were cool against her skin as Grace burrowed down, pulling the duvet up to her chin. She felt a thrill tingle through her, a heady mix of audacity and anticipation. This was what it felt like to be married, she was sure of it. Or at least, what she hoped it felt like. Maybe with more arguing about whose turn it was to take out the trash. She giggled softly, the sound muffled by the pillow. The wine was definitely kicking in. She closed her eyes, imagining Kyle's face when he emerged from the shower, expecting to find her primly waiting at the table with a polite smile. Instead, he'd find this. A pre-heated wife, ready and waiting.

A sudden, loud burst of off-key singing echoed from the bathroom. Grace's eyes snapped open. Okay, maybe the shower was lasting a little longer than expected. And that voice… dear Lord. Kyle was a terrible singer. She clamped a hand over her mouth to stifle another giggle. He sounded like a strangled cat being forced through a meat grinder. The singing abruptly stopped, replaced by the sound of the water being turned off. Grace's heart pounded against her ribs. Showtime.

Grace slipped out of the bed, slipped the shirt over her body and went back into the living room. It hung loosely on her frame, the hem reaching her mid-thigh, a silent declaration of her intent. She smoothed it down, trying to adopt a casual, alluring pose by the window, leaning back slightly, as if she'd just happened to be standing there in his shirt. The room was bathed in the soft, warm glow of the dimmed lights, making the apartment feel cozy and intimate.

The bathroom door creaked open, and Kyle stepped out, a towel slung low around his waist, water beading on his toned shoulders and chest. His hair was damp, and already starting to curl, and he looked... well, he looked good. He was rubbing his face with a smaller towel, still a little bleary from the wine, when his eyes landed on Grace. He froze. The towel paused mid-rub. His jaw, already slightly slack, dropped a fraction further. His gaze traveled from her bare legs, up the oversized tee, to her face, where a triumphant, slightly lopsided grin was playing. He blinked, slowly, then blinked again, as if trying to re-evaluate the reality unfolding before him.

"You look...different," Kyle finally managed, his voice a low rumble, still processing the image of Grace standing there in his shirt. "Is that...my shirt?" Grace giggled, a sound that was higher and a little more breathless than usual, thanks to the wine. "Maybe," she said, drawing out the word. He swallowed hard. "It...it suits you," he stammered, finally finding his voice. "But...how did you even...?" He trailed off, gesturing vaguely. "Never mind." He shook his head. "I'm going to get dressed before my towel falls off." He retreated

212

back into the bathroom, shaking his head and muttering under his breath.

A few minutes later, Kyle re-emerged from his room, now clad in pajama pants patterned with tiny pistols and a faded t-shirt that read "I <3 Bacon." He looked considerably less flustered, but still slightly bewildered. Grace was no longer by the window. She was now sitting on the couch, the controllers sitting next to her. "So," Kyle said, running a hand through his damp hair. "Game rematch?"

Grace nodded, a mischievous look in her eyes, and gestured for him to sit next to her. As he walked over, she watched as he grabbed his wine glass from the counter and sat down, carefully arranging his pistol-patterned pajama bottoms. He took a long sip, then picked up his controller, navigating through the menu to start the game again. Quickly, she jumped up, retrieving her own glass, then sat back down, this time, draping her legs over his lap.

Kyle froze, controller mid-air, his thumb hovering over the 'select character' button. His gaze dropped to her bare calves now resting comfortably over his lap, then slowly travelled up to the hem of his oversized gray t-shirt, which seemed to swallow her whole, yet simultaneously reveal just enough. He cleared his throat, a sound that came out more like a strangled squeak. "Uh... comfy?" he managed, trying to sound casual, but his voice was a little too high-pitched for his liking.

Grace just smiled, a sweet, innocent-looking tilt of her head that Kyle knew, from experience, usually preceded some form of delightful chaos. Her eyes, slightly glazed, sparkled with an impish gleam. "Very," she purred, leaning her head against his shoulder. "Now, are you going to pick Liu Kang and get your butt kicked again, or are we going to see some actual skill this time?"

The lights in the makeshift movie theater flickered on, illuminating the rows of comfortable chairs. David stood, stretching slightly, the credits of the movie rolling across the large screen. Jessica, nestled in his arms, sighed contentedly. "That was fun, Daddy. Thank you." David nuzzled her hair. "My pleasure, Baby." He carefully scooped her up in his arms, her petite frame feeling feather-light. Summer followed him out of the theater. "She looked like she had a good time, David." "She did," he replied, his voice low and soothing. "She needed a distraction from things."

He carried Jessica towards the stairs leading up to the main house. "Are you heading straight to bed?" Summer inquired, falling into step beside him. "Not quite yet," David responded, his gaze softening as he looked at Summer. He gently shifted Jessica in his arms, her head nestled against his shoulder. He knew Summer's subtle cues, the way her eyes held a deeper invitation when she spoke of bedtime. He paused at the foot of the stairs, turning slightly to face her.

"I have something else in mind first," he murmured, leaning down to press a soft, lingering kiss to Summer's lips. It was a kiss laden with all the care and foresight she admired in him, a silent promise of the intimacy they shared. Her lips parted slightly under his, a soft hum escaping her throat.

When he broke the kiss, he carried Jessica up the stairs, Summer following close behind, a faint blush on her cheeks.

He carefully brought Jessica to her room, gently laying her down in her bed and pulling the covers up around her. He brushed a strand of hair from her face, pressing a tender kiss to her forehead. "Sleep well, sweetheart," he whispered.

He then moved back out and walked with Summer to her room. As soon as they stepped inside, Summer immediately turned and firmly closed the door behind them, the soft click echoing in the quiet room. Her eyes, dark and inviting, met his as her fingers went to the hem of her shirt, pulling it up and over her head in one fluid motion. The soft light from the LCD window cast a faint light that seemed to make her skin glow, defining the graceful curve of her body. Her chest rose and fell with a quickened breath, a silent testament to the anticipation that now filled the room.

David's eyes, usually so sharp with calculation and planning, now held only warmth and desire as he watched her. A slow, knowing smile touched his lips, and he took a step closer, his hands reaching to gently cup her waist as she reached for the seam of his pants. Her skin was warm and soft against his palms, sending a shiver through her. He drew her closer, until her bare chest was pressed against his own, his gaze dropping to the swell of her breasts, a soft sigh escaping him.

"You're still so beautiful," he murmured, his voice a low, rough whisper that vibrated through her. He leaned in, his lips finding the delicate skin of her throat, tracing a path down to her collarbone. Her head tilted back, granting him more access, and her fingers wrapped around the back of his head, a soft groan escaping her. He worked his way down, his hands deftly unbuttoning the waistband of her shorts, sliding the denim down her hips. Summer lifted her legs slightly, helping him shed the last of her clothing, leaving her standing before him in nothing but the soft glow of the light.

He began his tender assault, his lips hot and insistent on her skin. He kissed her breasts, a gentle suckling motion that had her arching into him, her fingers digging into his shoulders. He lingered there, teasing and pleasuring, before moving lower, trailing wet kisses along her ribcage, down to her abdomen. His tongue danced over her navel, eliciting a sharp intake of breath from her, a delicious shiver running through her entire body. She gripped him tighter, her body swaying, completely lost in his touch.

His hands moved to her thighs, tracing the smooth skin, before his lips followed, pressing soft, reverent kisses along the inner curve of her leg. The intimacy of it sent a jolt through her, a wave of pure sensation that stole her breath. He knelt before her for a moment, his eyes full of adoration and fierce attraction.

Then, with a gentle hand, he turned her, guiding her to face away from him. Her back completely bare. He kissed her lower back, a trail of fire igniting her skin as his lips moved slowly, deliberately, over her spine, down to the small of her back. His hands slid around her waist, pulling her flush against his front, his breath warm on her ear.

"You've been such a good wife today," he murmured, his voice a low, rough rumble that vibrated through her, sending delicious tremors through her core. "I think you deserve a reward." Summer's mind reeled, her body already a quivering mess of sensation. Her thoughts were hazy with desire, but one clear, urgent thought broke through the fog. She leaned her head back against his shoulder, her voice barely a whisper, thick with longing.

"Would you… would you eat my pussy first, David?" she asked, the words a raw plea. She knew he would answer her deepest desires, always. A low chuckle vibrated through David's chest, a sound of pure delight and agreement. He didn't hesitate. With a surprising surge, he reached down, cupping her bottom, and then, in one smooth, powerful motion, lifted her. Summer gasped, her feet leaving the floor as he effortlessly propped her onto his shoulders.

Her head nearly reached the ceiling of the bedroom, the sudden shift in perspective disorienting, yet thrilling. She instinctively braced herself, her hands reaching up to steady herself against the cool, painted plaster. Her legs parted naturally with the movement, leaving her completely exposed, vulnerable, and exquisitely ready.

He moved slowly, deliberately, towards the corner of the room, the solid wall providing an anchor. The next moment was a blur of sensation. David, with his head thrown back, a look of pure, focused intensity on his face, devoured her. His mouth was hot, wet, and utterly insatiable against her. He pressed her against the wall, her back firm against the cool surface, as his tongue worked wonders, swirling and stroking, teasing and pleasuring, with a precision that bordered on surgical, yet was filled with a primal hunger that made her tremble intensely.

Every nerve ending in her body screamed, alive and buzzing with an intensity she always savored. She grasped the wall, her knuckles white, her body rigid with a pleasure so profound it bordered on pain. The world narrowed to the wet heat of his mouth, the insistent pressure, the dizzying height, the unyielding wall behind her.

Then, without warning, the climax hit her. It was instantaneous, a volcanic eruption that seized her entire being. A guttural cry ripped from her throat as she arched violently against the wall, her body seizing with wave after wave of intense pleasure. She came, and came, and came, the orgasm so powerful, so immediate, that it poured out of her in an undeniable gush. She felt the warm, slick wetness run down David's chin, and along her legs, a tangible sign of her complete surrender, and then drip, drip, drip onto the tile floor below.

Her legs trembled, threatening to give way even as David held her steady. Her breath came in ragged gasps, her mind blissfully blank save for the echo of pure, unadulterated pleasure. He continued to taste her, to lick away the evidence of her release, his commitment to her pleasure absolute. Summer clung to the wall, her strength momentarily gone, her body still vibrating with the aftershocks of her intense orgasm.

David slowly released her, a mischievous look in his eyes. He watched her fall, catching her by the thighs before she hit the ground, his hands strong and unwavering. "David!" Summer gasped, breathless and flushed, a playful scold in her voice, even as she clung to him. "You almost let me drop!" He chuckled. "Almost," he agreed. "But I would never let you fall, my Dear. Never."

Then, as he looked her in the eye, that familiar, intense gaze that seemed to peel back every layer of her soul, he slowly, deliberately slid his cock inside of her. Summer was still very sensitive, her nerves alight from the recent, overwhelming climax. The initial thrust, though gentle, was a shock to her exquisitely tender core, and she gasped, a small, involuntary squirt dampening his thigh, a testament to her heightened arousal. Still trembling slightly, her body a live wire humming with residual pleasure and renewed anticipation, Summer murmured, her voice almost inaudible, "Hurt me."

David's eyes widened slightly, a spark of pure understanding igniting within their depths. He knew. He knew exactly what she meant. She wasn't asking for pain, not in the literal sense. She was asking for oblivion, for a pleasure so profound, so all-consuming, that it would push her to the very precipice of consciousness, until she surrendered completely, utterly, to him and the sensations he would unleash. She meant: "fuck me until I pass out, don't stop, don't slow down." It was her desire to be utterly dominated by him, to lose herself completely.

A primal hum vibrated deep in David's chest, a response to her profound vulnerability and fierce demand. His grip on her thighs tightened, steadying her as he began to move, a slow, deliberate thrust that filled her completely. He felt her clench around him, a sweet, irresistible vice. The air in the bedroom grew thick with their combined heat and musk, the rhythmic slap of skin against skin becoming the only sound that mattered.

He pulled back, almost to the brink of escaping her, and then plunged back in, deeper, firmer. Summer cried out, a guttural sound that was half pleasure, half plea. Her fingers, still clutching the wall for support, dug into the plaster, then slid down to grip his shoulders, her nails pressing into his skin, an anchor in the maelstrom of sensation. Each thrust was an arrow finding its mark, piercing through the lingering aftershocks of her previous climax, igniting new, exhilarating fires.

David watched her, his gaze unwavering. He saw the flicker of her eyelashes, the slight tremor that started in her legs and climbed through her body, the way her head lolled back against the wall, exposing the graceful line of her throat. He felt the rapid flutter of her heart against his chest as he enclosed her in his arms, pressing her closer, abandoning the wall altogether. Now, she was suspended entirely by him, her legs wrapped around his waist, her core riding against his with every powerful stroke.

"Yes," she whimpered, a breathless whisper against his ear. "Like that, David. Don't... don't stop." He wouldn't. He couldn't. Her complete surrender fueled him, transforming his dominance into an act of profound commitment. He varied the angle, the depth, finding her most sensitive spots with unerring precision, driving her higher and higher. Her squirming, her gasps, the way her body convulsed around him, it was all the affirmation he needed. He felt his own pleasure building, a powerful wave that he held meticulously in check, focused entirely on her. This was for Summer, a gift of pure sensation, a transcendental experience that would blot out the world.

Her breaths became shallower, more ragged, punctuated by sharp, involuntary cries. Her body, already depleted, was now being pushed to its limits. Her muscles spasmed, a beautiful, uncontrolled dance of pure bliss. He could feel her beginning to fade, her limbs growing heavy, her awareness narrowing to the exquisite friction of their joined bodies. David leaned down, kissing her forehead, her temple, her lips, tasting the salt and sweetness of her skin. "You're almost there, my love," he murmured, his voice a low rumble against her ear, spurring her on. He wasn't asking if she was ready; he was guiding her, firmly yet tenderly, over the edge.

With one final, deep thrust, David felt Summer's entire body lock. A long, drawn-out moan escaped her, a sound of utter release and profound exhaustion. Her eyes rolled back for a moment, her head falling against his shoulder, her breath caught in her throat. She convulsed around him, her core clenching, milking him dry as wave after wave, even more intense than the one before, washed over her. Her grip on him went limp, her body boneless against his.

David held her close, his own cum a powerful, searing rush that mirrored hers, pouring into her as she trembled. When it was over, she was a dead weight in his arms, her breathing shallow, her body slick with sweat and their shared fluids. He carefully lifted her, carrying her to her bed, laying her gently on the cool, soft sheets. He pulled the light blanket over her, then lay beside her, gathering her into his arms.

Appendix: 1

Seth

Bonnie

Kyle

Grace

Callie

Reagan

Emma

www.ingramcontent.com/pod-product-compliance
Lightning Source LLC
Chambersburg PA
CBHW051949220626
47052CB00004B/859